The Game
of
Fire & Ice

Flairs and Glairs
Publication House

“The Game of Fire and Ice”

ISBN No: " 978-93-91302-65-8"
1st Edition
Language – English and Hindi

Flairs and Glairs
Publication House
Regd. Under MSME Act.

Disclaimer

This is a work of fiction and solely represent the thoughts of the corresponding authors of the articles. Our editors have tried their best to edit the content of all the authors and check the plagiarism.

All the write-ups in this book are unique and are only published in this book.

In case any plagiarism or error is found, only the author is responsible alone, and not the publisher or the Compilers.

Cover Designing and Book Formatting

Shubham Shah and Ishani Agarwal

Acknowledgement

Dear Almighty, thank you for blessing me with the power and zeal to be able to complete this Anthology.

Also, Thank You dear parents, for trusting in me, and letting me work whenever I wanted. My family is the one who supported me for what I am today.

When it comes to this, Anthology, I would like to start with Thanking the Co -Authors, without your help and support, I would have never been able to complete it.

Thank you all of you, for being there. Much Love to all of you. I am glad to see you all standing by me.

Co Author

Shubham Shah (Founder Flairs and Glairs)
Ishani Agarwal (Co-Founder Flairs and Glairs)
Shivangi Jaiswal (Compiler)

1. Jyoti Singh Rajput
2. Vineet Verma
3. Shubhangi Shekhar
4. Shyam Swank
5. Rinkle Dudhani
6. Sandeep Rajput
7. Reena Kadam
8. Prasad Babu Galla
9. Payal Indani
10. Pooja J. Indani
11. Dr Shreeja Singh Chandel
12. Neha Gupta
13. Sunita Bajaj
14. Nikeeta Das
15. Farhan Rahman
16. Nikhil Jain
17. Moaliba Singh
18. Bhumi Maheshkumar Gupta
19. Vrinda
20. Ritu Sharma
21. Shivani Brijesh
22. Arpit Dubey
23. Samragyee Basak
24. Potula Sai Srilekha

25. Aaliyah Stark
26. Kamalpreet Singh
27. Amit Kumar Paswan
28. Uddhav Kanhai
29. Shrawasthi Sontakke
30. Riya Shailendrasingh Thakur
31. Ankit
32. Neeraj Baswal
33. Riya Jumariya
34. Shilpa Vaishnav
35. Shivam Chowdhary
36. Alfiya Suroor Khan
37. Kreesha Kothari
38. Ankush Chauhan
39. Chetan
40. Sonal Singh

Shubham Shah

(Founder- Flairs and Glairs)

Shubham Shah, an entrepreneur at "Flairs & Glairs" a brand with dynamics in events organizing and cultural educational pan INDIA, is a 26yrs old guy who recently has entered the digital platform of imprinting emotions. He has initiated with his own open mic platform to help budding poets and aspiring writers under his brand named as "Teekhe Zasbaaat"

He is a commerce graduate from the Bhagalpur City of Bihar. He states Writing has impersonated him since childhood and he has now been writing for over a decade!

Cooking, on the other hand, is his passion! He also mentions, trying out new things just tickles him!

When asked sir, Why SPICY EMOTIONS?

He smiled and added, "agar jasbaat teekhe na ho toh wo jasbaat kahan" Spices are all that blends! So do his words!

As a chef, he presents to you his dish! Hot and freshly served! Taste it! Feel it! Enjoy it! You can also find his writing in the Book "Teekhe Zasbaaat" and 50+ Co -authored anthologies.

With his passion to explore opportunities across Platforms, he is working with keen dev otion and We wish him all the very best for his future ventures.

He is Featured in the International Magazine DeMode for his upcoming solo novel.

He is Approved by Ne8x for its Lit Fest, and is a Golden Star Awards 2020 Winner.

He is a India Book of Records Holder for his Anthology Satrang, and has the Grandmaster title by Asia Book of Records, for the same.

He has also been featured in Prabhat Khabar, Dainik Jagran, and a lot of other Newspapers in Bihar for his achievements.

He has been a proud co-author to

India Book Of Records (Title- Black)

World Book Of Records (Title -15 Wonders of Poetries)

India Book Of Records (Title - Aaina)

Vajra World Records Holder (Title - Gustakhi Maaf Hai)

High Range of Records Holder (Title - Gustakhi Maaf Hai)

Indian Book of Records

(Title - Road from Worst to Best)

Share your reviews on his

INSTAGRAM

@spicy_emotions
@shubham4shah

Or via email on

shubham2shah@gmail.com

To stay tuned to his work and opportunities follow his business Handles

INSTAGRAM FACEBOOK YOUTUBE

@flairsandglairs
@teekhezasbaaat

WEBSITE:

https://flairsandglairs.in/
https://flairsandglairs.com/

Ishani Agarwal

(Co-Founder- Flairs and Glairs)

Ishani Agarwal hails from the City of Joy, Kolkata.
She is the co -founder of her Community "Teekhe Zasbaaat" and Flairs and Glairs Publication.
Been a Compiler for 45+ Anthologies, she is in the process for more. Co-authored in 150+ Anthologies. She is a India Book of Records Holder, a Vajra World Records Holder, a High Range of Records Holder, an OMG Book of Records Holder, a Bravo Record holder, a Forever Star Book of World Records and an Indian Book of Records Holder.
Approved by Ne8x for its Lit Fest 2020, and Literary Icon 2020. Also a Golden Star Awards Winner 2020.
She has also been award ed with India Star Republic Award 2021, a part of She Awards by Awards Arc and Winner of Nari Samman 2021 by Literoma.

She is also selected as Best Achiever of the Year by AwardsArc and Most Challenging Compiler Award by Spectrum Awards.
She got her first solo Published,a solo Compilation consisting of first 750 contents of hers, titled "Hand That Burnt While Healing".

She has been featured by the National Magazine "Taree Zameen Par" with the title 'unstoppable'.
Also featured in the International Magazine DeMode for her upcoming solo novel, she is proud to write on social issues, and is happy with the love she is receiving.
Connect with her on Instagram: @Ishani_agarwal_quotes / @compilations_so_far

Shivangi Jaiswal
(Compiler)

Shivangi Jaiswal is a Content Writer from Kolkata. Executive Head at “Flairs & Glairs” brand with dynamics in events organizing and cultural educational pan INDIA. Organizer at "The Glittering Fables" Writing Community. She is a B. Com Honors graduate. Certified in Stocks & Short Selling as well as Certified in Digital Marketing student.
She is an Indian Book of Record Holder.

Approved by Ne8x for its Lit Fest 2020 for the Author of the Year 2020 and the Real Hero's Title 2020. Also, a Warrior of Change Awardee 2021.
Recently been awarded Writer of the year Award 2021 by Forever Star World book of Records.
She loves to bring smiles and happiness to many faces, so she is into social service.
Traveler, Teacher, Meditator, Dancer, Singer, Instrument Player. She loves to play guitar and harmonium. Also been awarded in many events for winning many categories Been a Public Speaker she has taken part in many events and nailed it. Been a great Advisor to many. She has also been crowned for winning Miss Great Podium 2020 Title in the category Modelling recently. Sports freakof Swimming and Badminton with a passion so strong. Since, past one year she has started her writing journey.
She writes so that many people can connect with their stories and get positive hopes. She thinks " Every story is unique so embrace yourself to the best". She is a writer by day and a reader by night. Been a Complier of 40+ Anthologies, and in process for more, also Co - authored 1 50+ anthologies. Shivangi is an old soul with young eyes, a vintage heart, and a beautiful mind."

You can follow her work:
Instagram
@the_knockingvibe
@house_of_compilations

Trapped Pain.

I wear a smile,
which is empty inside.
Leaving it back behind the past.
Not knowing about the future.

Crying inside,
But no one could see my tears.
All I wanted was you near me.
But I feel I'm tied up with chains
Trapped all around in a box
Not knowing the way out to go.

It's painful
It's hurtful
It's tearing me inside
It's killing me.
I need you to be here with me.

This pain is taking its toll
But my love for you will never get old.
A painful misery keeps on going.
From love to pain.
I will always be painfully in love with you.

Fire & Ice Love.

A deadly combination of fire and ice.

He is fire, she is cold as ice.

Every one said: How come they are
still together?

Unaware of the fact that one smile of her calms down the fire inside him.

And one touch of him melts her cold heart.

Such of power of love between them

That no one could break it.

Everyone could see destruction, but only few could see the everlasting bond they have.

One Wish.

If God would grant me one wish,
I would love to fly high and touch the sky.

Flying with wings in beauty, like the butterfly in the sky;
Climbing the cloud and starry skies.

And all that's best of
I would meet the real me dancing in happiness & joy.

Which heaven has granted me?
One shade of more happiness, one ray of hope.

The smiles, the tiny glow, the gracefulness
How pure, how vivid their dwelling place.

Breaking all the strings,
And making dreams come true.

I fly high all day and night
Believe in yourself, you are born with wings.

Be A Healer.

If one can stop someone from
stepping into thc world of thorns.
She shall never go in vain.

If one can erase someone's life scars,
And make it heal.
She will live a new life.

If one can help someone to not shink
and settle,
The sea will never have any storm.

Everything falls in a shower, don't
dissolve in it.
Rather Solve and Survive in it.

Jyoti Singh Rajput

Jyoti Singh Rajput is a banker by profession and marks the ink, as her passion. She believes, the pen holded with passion, has power to bring change and it even emote the emotions, that can't be verbally exchanged and are left unsaid. She is also a lyricist, a nature lover, an enthusiast contributing to welfare works and urges all to help those who needs, as she says, we are human for good deeds. A multilingual and a promising poet, Jyoti Singh Rajput has worked in many books of different genres. She is a basket of masterpieces and her poetry sheds stories, some of love and the stirring memories, some of glories and the waving worries, some of life and it's theories. You can follow her on instagram @ t he_frozen_flame_2801, and on yourquote @ Jyoti- the frozen flame for her more write ups.

है फिर इक बार जज़्बात जगी
सांसों को फिर तेरी तलब लगी...

है फिर इक बार जज़्बात जगी
सांसों को फिर तेरी तलब लगी
दस्तक जो तूने महफ़िल में दी
धड़कन में है हलचल सी मची
बीते लम्हों की है आंधी चली
कुछ यादों की बरसात गिरी
दिल में फिर वही चाह भरी
रूठे सपनों को है राह मिली
तेरी आस में थी जो शाम ढली
आज रौशन उसकी गली गली
सर्द रातें अब है सुलग रही
मन मचल रहा हर घड़ी घड़ी
है फिर इक बार जज़्बात जगी
सांसों को फिर तेरी तलब लगी...

She Was Fading With Every Moonlight

Though, she seems happy in daylight
But she misses him in the dark, quiet night
She craves for those cute, lusty fight
But sleeps, holding those lovely memories, tight
She prays for things to be alright
Wishes, one day he will call her, his love, his pride
And the engulfing silence between them, will break
Those furled feelings will recollide
The heart will bloom and the love will pour its light
And the life will again sing and indite
But, with passing of days, her hopes, her dreams bright,
We're drowning in that blacklight
And tired of hiding and fighting the pain inside
She screams and cries
As the destiny betrays to unite
She was left with emptiness, lonliness, in every moonlight
Slowly, she faded and her desire died
Awaiting the love, the delight
And so called her mr right...

Vineet Verma

He is Vineet Verma, from Bulandshahr U.P., pursuing Business Management studies. Having too much interest in writing because of having knowledge of words and because of one-sided love also .If you like his shayris.do follow him on Instagram @shayr_v21.

"चलो आज जुदा हो जाते हैं

हम आपके बुरे ख्वाब से और आप हमारे खुदा हो जाते हैं
मयस्सर मुकम्मल मोहब्बत नहीं है
ना हमें ना तुम्हें
चलो आज यूंही बेवजह खो जाते हैं
हम आपकी गोद में सोते हैं और आपसे अलविदा हो जाते हैं
चलो आज जुदा हो जाते हैं"1

"सोचा था
सोचा था मेरी बाहों में घर होगा तेरा,
सोचा था हर सफर में हमसफ़र होगा तू मेरा,
ना पता था, "ना" मिलेगी मोहब्बत के इज़हार के बदले मुझको
ना पता था, "ना" मिलेगी कभी तू मुझको,
चलो खैर छोड़ो,
बस सोचा ही तो था,
बहुत कुछ सोचा था।"2

"तुम्हारे मिनजानिब तोड़े गए मेरे दिल को मैं संभाल लूंगा
बाखुदा अपनी इबारत से ही तुम्हें मैं सज़ा दूंगा"3

"तुम्हारा दिल तो मेरा हो ना सका, पर मेरा तो तुम रख लो
तुम्हारी खुशियों में मैं मेहमान ना सही, पर मेरी खुशियां तो तुम रख लो
हां, मेरे आंसू, जो तुम्हारे लिए ही बहते हैं, बस उन्हें मेरे रहने दो
बाकि सब कुछ जिसपर मेरा हक है, मेरे महबूब के हक से, तुम रख लो"4

"दूर तलक देखो ज़रा, कोई नूर आया है
खुदा के दर से उतर कर एक हूर आया है

तलब लगा दें आंखें जिसकी, ऐसी बला का सुरूर आया है
नज़र सम्भालिएगा ज़रा, आज मुद्दतों बाद मेरा हुज़ूर आया है"5

"एक शायर होना पता है क्या है...
हर खुबसूरत लगती चीज़ में तुम्हें देखना
और तुम्हारे बारे में कुछ लिख देना
फिर चाहे वो तुम्हारी तारीफें हों या तुम्हारी मेरी मोहब्बत से बेरूखी"6

"मेरे लबों पर पहरा है तेरा
ना जाने तुझ पर ही आकर क्यूं ठहरा है दिल मेरा
जुनून है कुछ अलग ही तेरी चाहत में, तेरी इबादत में
तू साथ हो तो उजाला है, तेरे सिवा बस अंधेरा है मेरा"7

"शायद तेरे सबसे करीब होकर भी तुझसे सबसे दूर हूं
प्यार करने को तुझे मजबूर हूं, जो ना करूं प्यार तुझसे तो मैं बेमतलब बेफिज़ूल हूं
मोहब्बत मेरी नहीं बल्कि मैं मोहब्बत का गुरूर हूं
तू साथ हो, पास हो, मेरी हो या ना हो पर मैं तेरा ज़रूर हूं"8

तेरी मोहब्बत में शायर बनकर अब और नहीं जीना मुझे
तेरी नाकुबूलगी का ख़ामियाज़ा अपने सीने में अब और नहीं सीना मुझे
तेरी मुस्कराहट की चमक बार-बार याद दिला कर अब तो चिढ़ाता है मेरी अंगूठी का भी नगीना मुझे
तेरी यादों का कूली बनकर अपने आंसूओं का नमक अब और नहीं पीना मुझे
तेरी मोहब्बत में शायर बनकर अब और नहीं जीना मुझे"9

"झकझोर कर रख देती हैं मुझे मेरी ही उम्मीदें
जो मैं तुमसे लगाए बैठा हूं

चाहकर भी कोई और पसंद ही नहीं आती
आखिर....दिल जो मैं तुमसे लगाए बैठा हूं"10

"ना जाने क्यूं पर
तुम्हारी आदत सी हो गई है,
यारी तुमसे हुई
और खुद ही से अदावत सी हो गई है,
गलतफहमियां है बड़ी दिल में दबी झूठी उम्मीदों पर
भंवर सा उठा है दिल में, ना जाने कैसी आफ़त सी हो गई है,
ध्वस्त हुआ अब दिल मेरा
और लोग कहते हैं कि ज़माने से मेरी बगावत सी हो गई है...."11

"शायद हर पल के साथ घट रही हर घटना के पीछे कुछ वजह होती है
और
शायद वही झूठ है जिसे खुद से बोलकर मैं अपनी अधूरी मोहब्बत को सही मान लेता हूं"12
2020

31 dec 2019 की वो रात
क्या सोचा था किसी ने कि सुबह होते ही
प्रकृति बदले के सिलसिले के एक नये सूरज के साथ आएगी
आम आदमी, पशु पक्षी और यहां तक की सितारों तक को खा जाएगी
वसूल करेगी खुद पर हुए लाखों ज़ुल्मो सितम को ब्याज लगाकर
कभी आग, कभी कोरोना तो कभी यूंही बेमौत बुला कर
चूर करेगी इंसान के सारे घमंड और अहंकार वो
सुनेगी जब अपने क़ातिलों की चीख-पुकार वो
पल भर में सबको अपनी गोद में समां लेगी
कुछ यूं वो हम सब से हिसाब लेगी
किराएदार हैं मानव मालिक नहीं उसके

बहुत हुआ अब..वापस ले लेगी सब कुछ वो, लायक नहीं हम जिसके......

31 dec 2019 की वो रात
क्या सोचा था किसी ने

Shubhangi Shekhar

She's a student and loves to explore new opportunities She also only express her feelings in way of poetry because कहते हैं ना ख़ामोशियाँ ही दिल की बात बयां करती है!!!

बलात्कार!!!

जानता था कलयुग आएगा।
क्या इंसान इतना बदल जाएगा,
जिस बच्ची के आँखों में मासूमियत है
क्या उसे ही देख किसी का हैवानियत जाग जाएगा,
दरिंदों की तरह जब तूने उसे छुआ होगा
क्या तेरा रूह नहीं कांपा होगा,
एक बार तो उसकी आँखों में देख
क्या तुझे अपनी बहन - बेटी याद नहीं आयी होगी,
उसकी दर्द भरी चीख सुन
क्या तुझे खुद पर शर्म नहीं आयी होगी,
कैसे तू उस रात सोया होगा
क्या तुझे खुद से नफ़रत नहीं हुई,
ऐ दरिंदें!!! ज़रा आईने में देख
खुद से नज़रे भी नहीं मिला पाएगा,
तुझे देख तो ईश्वर भी शर्मिंदा होगा
क्यूँ इस दरिन्दे को उसने धरती पर भेजा होगा!!!!

बचपन के वो दोस्त!!!

याद है मुझे बचपन के वो दोस्त,
जिनके साथ करते थे हम मौज,
हम कहने को तो तीन थे,
मगर जहां जाते वहाँ धूम मचाते थे,
किसके घर खाते,
किसके घर सोते,
हमे ये भी ना पता होता,
हम दोस्त नहीं,
परिवार से बढ़ कर थे,
मगर सब अलग हो गए,
बहुत ढूँढा नहीं मिले,
काश हम फिर कहीं मिले,
फिर वही मस्ती करे,
और दोहराए अपना बचपन....

Shyam Swank

This is Shyam swank. A guy highly inspired for Indian Armed Forces. Being a cadet at Sainik School Nalanda he doesn't get a lot of time for allthese sorts of creativity, but he has tried his level best. This story is just his imagination...Hope u like it...

Yes, I Still Do Regret

Have you ever wondered what hurts you the most that constantly keeps killing you from your within? I strongly believe it's repentance, being sorry to yourself or reverse of something that you had a better opportunity to do. If this statement sounds unrealistic or impractical to you then I would recommend you to recall the moment from movie 3 idiots Aamir Khan saying "Farhan! aaj se 40 saal baad tu aise hi kisi hospital mein pada hoga toh sochega yaar! uss samay thodi si himmat kar leta toh life kuch aur hoti"

So, here goes the same this is me, Vivaan feeling pretty much like hopeless, every single moment irks me with a bulk of regrets whenever I try to delete my feelings for her there is always an error & hang pretty much like in jio phone because my love, care and feelings for her has always been boundless and endless which would go beyond infinity. Perhaps words would never be enough to express this saddned part of me.

So this all started when I joined coaching classes in 11th standard, this coachin g was indeed magnificent and vulnerable. I am really terrible at Biology, memorizing all those stuff and terms always seemed like out of my league. So, like always I was kicked out of the class for not completing my signment with some of my friends who wee far more clear not to opt science but you know how tough it is something like next to impossible to convince Indian parents. The only thing we would do outside the class is cursing bio teacher & enjoying the panoramic view.
Out of the blue, I saw a very beautiful girl wearing a cordial smile that took her beauty to another level walking towards us with our headmaster sir, so it was a new admission. I was called by headmaster said to take her to "11th A" she is Aisha headmaster sir said.

Me: Hii, Aisha this is Vivaan.
Aisha: Hlo, but why were you outside the class??
Me: Actually, we are sort of extraordinary guys, we always complete our assignments on time that's why we are outside enjoying this panoramic view.
She started laughing and I must admit she had the most wonderful laugh. Then, I told her I am not good at this subject that's why I was thrown out of the class. Our conversation continued till we reached to our classroom, she agreed to give me her notes saying it would help me to understand better. Lastly I tend to ask her Instagram ID saying in case I need to thank you for this and guess what again a cordial smile.

This is how our conversation began we started sharing our thoughts, views and ideas and we became very much understanding to each other. we shared each other's childhood ex- boyfriend, ex girlfriend, crushes, films, foods, sports, BJP, Congress everything. Perhaps nothing was off the topic with her and talking to her was the most beautiful feelings for me bcz..I never felt judged.

when I talk about my root I had my ex studying in same coaching because of some misunderstandings we split up, we tried to fix it but it could not be, we both needed our own space, so splitting up was better option we both agreed to.

Me and Aisha it was all going well there was not even a single day, I slept without having a conversation with her. So, one day at the end with saying good night I hesitantly sent 3 kiss emoticons, I knew it was a creep behaviour but after waiting for a few seconds whichfelf like hours, I received 3 emoticons from her, wow. genuinely I felt like on the top of the world & the whole world is under my feet.

After a point of time I could realise that she's the one I shall hold her hand to infinity and in fact beyond infinity. But the question that revolved around my mind was "will it be an appropriate time?" I was afraid of being judged and I didn't want to lose her at any cost so I could not muster courage to speak my heart out, my feelings to her.
Aisha was going through the same mystery like if she proposes first she would probably come between me and my ex, so she never express her feelings. After all these stuffs a point came she felt like I might not have feelings for her, so she accepted the proposal from a boy named Raj who consta ntly followed, loved and cared for her. This was all cleared out on the occasion of teacher's day, hats off to the one who discovered the game "Truth and Dare" she confessed her feelings. And I ended up having a bulk of regrets.

So, with a very heavy heart, This Vivaan wants to give a message to the whole universe that if you have genuine feelings for someone, if someone's happiness is the only thing that matters to you. Then its humble and sincere requesto "Go ahead with a very optimistic thought" justspeak your heart out so that you don't end up having a bulk of regrets or this sort of dark phase in your life.say it before it is too late...

Rinkle Dudhani

Rinkle is a 2nd year law student who started writing since a very young age, she finds poem writing very soothing. Whenever she's confused or can't express herself to anyone, she jot downs her thoughts. she also has her interest in 'nature photography'.

Think Over

How fast all of this is going,
All of us are surviving and not living.
Everyone is smiling but nobody is happy,
Give it a thought, you'll definitely find it wacky!
Can't we stop for a second and breathe,
Stop being a sword in a sheath.
Can't we do a little care,
Be like a feather floating with the air.
Can't we hear the silence,
End the noise and create some balance,
How fast all of this is going,
We are just surviving and not living.
Let's stop running, start staying.
Stop struggling, start slaying.
Stop pretending, start understanding.
Stop surviving, start living.
Let's make an attempt to go slow,
let happiness outshine and I hope then, we all will be just fine.

Tart Or Traitor?

I've been called love, moon, babe, darling
just to get called at the end, a bitch
because they think I ditched.

I never asked them to love me, I've always been a free dove
it was their choice to kill our friendship with that arrow of love

I didn't fall, was that my fault?
everyone said the same words "I love you"
I believed all of them,
if I'd have chosen one, i'd be a traitor
if I'd have chosen all, i'd be a tart.

We Don't Get Along!

You and me, me and you, we don’t get along.

Once your voice used to be my fav song,
Now it annoys me if i hear it for long.

Once i couldnt bear to stay away from you,
Now i dont like being near you.

Once your touch used to give me thrill,
Now even the thought of it gives me chills.

Once you were a beautiful dream of mine,
Now you are nothing but a nightmare with no shine.

Once i used to be in love with you from the core,
I still love you but unfortunately i don’t like you anymore.

You and me, me and you, we don't get along.

Captivating Strangers

Each morning, sitting in my balcony
I see people passing by,
some, in joy
and some, in melancholy.
I see people who are utterly strangers to me,
Yet, their presence in that moment, right in front of me, seems absolutely rare to me!
That old man, wearing a pink tshirt with green shoes couldn't be more carefree!
That lady, holding her son's hand, is sad low-key!
That man walking slowly might be thinking, what will be, will be!
That you don't need to be big in order to fly high, a little bird told me!
Each morning, sitting in my balcony
I see people passing by,
people who are strangers to me,
strangers who are strange, yet captivating to me.

Sandeep Rajput

15-year-old Sandeep Rajput just entered 10th class, studying in Jawahar Navodaya Vidyalaya, Panipat

They are very interested in writing along with their studies, today they try to write this, due to lack of special attention in Hindi, they had a lot of problems, later when they were fond of writing, they gradually the nuances of words started to go Today, he is able to express the words of our mind in words.

(1)

वो सजकर खुद को सजाकर आई मैं देखता रह गया
वो हाथों में मेहंदी लगा कर आई मैं देखता रह गया

सके निगाहों में दर्द, अश्क, बरकरार थे
फिर कैसे नज़रें झुकाकर आई मैं देखता रह गया

मुझे मालूम है मुझसे दो गुना दर्द उसे हो रहा था
मगर वो ऐसे दर्द छुपा कर आई मैं देखता रह गया

फांसी :एक आसान मौत

रास्ते फिर निगलने लगे बहनों, बेटियों को
कौन से दरिंदे खड़े हैं रास्तों पर
क्या कर रही है सरकार कहां है कानून
वही कानून जो बिक जाते हैं रास्तों पर

हमारी बहनें हमारी बेटियां हैं
हमें रुकना नहीं है अब आगे आने के लिए
कुछ पहल कुछ कदम उठाने पड़ेंगे
हमारी बहनों बेटियों को बचाने के लिए

फांसी मत दो इन दरिंदों को
यह तो आसान मौत होगी
उखाड़ फीकवा दो उस अंग को
जिसके दम पर दरिंदे कूदते हैं
नोच लो उन आंखों को
जिससे वह बहन बेटियों को घूरते हैं
कटवा दो उन हाथों को
जिससे उन्होंने बहनों को छुआ है
बदल दो उन सड़कों को रास्तों को
जहां यह घिनौना काम हुआ है
कटवाने चाहिए वो पांव भी
पीछे पड़ जाते हैं वो बहनों के

इस गंदगी को मिटाना पड़ेगा हमें ही
कब तक एक के बाद एक की बारी होगी
आज उसकी बहन ,बेटी थी उस जगह पर
कल क्या पता हमारी या तुम्हारी होगी

(3)

बातें हल्की-हल्की तुम क्या बोलते हो
समझ नहीं आता जितनी दफा बोलते हो
क्या सच में सच से रुबरु कराओगे हमें
यार संदीप तुम झूठ बड़ा बोलते हो

(4)

दुका°-ए-इश्क अगर बाजार में लगा दोगे
इश्क देने लगे तो कैसे और क्या दोगे
अगर मैं तैयार हो भी जाऊं लेने को
धोखा नहीं मिलेगा क्या इतना बता दोगे

Reena Kadam

अमावस्या

गर्द त्या अंधाऱ्या राती
काजव्यांची सोबत होती
तुला शोधायला निघाले मी
पण वाट अनवाणी होती
तुझ्या गालावर पडणारी ती खळी
त्या चंद्रात असणाऱ्या लोभस डागाची आठवण करून देत होती
मग त्याच अंधारात शोधायला निघाले मी तो चंद्र
मग कळलं त्या रात्री तर अमावस्या होती

आरसा

ती तुझा प्रवास होती
पण तु माझा शोध होतास
ती तुझ्यासाठी समुद्राची लहर होती
पण तु माझ्यासाठी त्या सागराचा किनारा होतास
तिच्यापासून लांब जाण्याचे कधी कधी बहाणे शोधतोस तु
पण तुला मी कधी कळू नाही दिलं की तु माझ्यासाठी किती खास होतास
आज ती तुझ्यासाठी तुझं प्रतिबिंब आहे
पण तु मात्र माझ्यासाठी नेहमी माझा आरसा होतास

बेघर

रेव ती त्या किनाऱ्यावरची
आणि तिच्यातच निसटून जात होतास तु
स्पर्श तर होतं होता तुला त्या लाटेचा
तरीही तुटून जात होतास तु
मनात खूप काही साचलं होतं तुझ्या
पण व्यक्त मात्र होतं न्हवतास
किनाऱ्यावर सुंदर ते घर होतं तुझं तिथे
आणि तरीही तु बेघर होतास

बरखास्त

सुरांची मैफिल ती बसली होती ऐनवेळी
पण मनाची तार माझ्या निसटून गेली होती
जुडणारा असूनही जुळत न्हवती ती तार मनाची
म्हणून अशीच गंजून पडून गेली होती
एक दिवस तुटली ती तार माझ्या मनाची जेव्हा
जेव्हा गात होता सगरम तिच्यासाठी
आणि मैफिल माझी बरखास्त करून टाकली होती

दिशाहीन

सुगंध देणाऱ्या झाडाच फुल नको मला
तु चालत असलेल्या कांट्यावरून चालायला मी तयार आहे
तो निरागस भासणारा किनारा नको मला
तु वाहत असलेल्या पुरात मी वाहायला तयार आहे
अंगावरून वाहणारी वाऱ्याची झुळूक नको मला
तु धडपडत असलेल्या वादळात अडकायला मी तयार आहे
मग तु जाशील त्या दिशेला मी माझं समजेन
कारण आयुष्यभर तुझ्यासोबत दिशाहीन होण्यासाठी मी तयार आहे

सुगावा

पाहावं की बेनजर व्हावं
तुझ्यात जुरावं की असंच मरून जावं
तुझ्यावर चिडून राहावं की तुझ्याशी बोलावं
सुचत नाही जेव्हा
तेव्हा वाटतं डोळे बंद करून कायमच झोपून जावं
सुगावा नाही तुझा कसला
ना तुला फिकीर माझी
म्हणून आता कळतं नाही निघुन जावं की अजून थोडं थांबावं

नातं

काय आहे नातं तुझ्या माझ्यातलं
जे अंधाऱ्या राती निखळून येणारं
न्हवती गरज मला त्या तुझ्या शरीराच्या स्पर्शाची
कारण शब्दाच्या मिठीत हृदय केव्हाच गुंतलं होतं
नसेल कधीच साथ आपली आयुष्यभरासाठी
पण स्वप्नातल्या प्रवासात मात्र तु नेहमी माझ्या सोबत असावं

खंत

जाताना ती अशी सहज निघुन गेली
कित्येक वर्षाची वेळ अशी तोडून गेली ती
किती काळ असतो मधला ह्याचा आभास नाही तिला
सोपं नसतं सगळं काही विसरून नव्याने जगायला
खंत मनात एकच उरली होती की मी कुठे कमी पडलो
जेणेकरून ती सहज दुसऱ्याच्या मिठीत सामावून गेली

Prasad Babu Galla

Prasad Babu Galla, 30 years old, belongs to Visakhapatnam. He pursued bachelor's degree and aims to become a successful author. He is in part of above 30 anthologies yet to be published and aims for record of 2021 anthologies in this year 2021. He loves writing about Love and Inspirational Stories. To reach him, you can contact on his personal Instagram handle @prasadbabugalla, Your Quote @prasadbabugalla and email id babuprasad20@gmail.com

Ace of Hearts

All enchants, thoughts and emotions
whatever whips in my heart frames
are all my dictators of Love
to feed thousands of flames.

I wake up from my dreams
to spend that happy hour
with you in the midnight
when I am beside the pillar.

You are my moonshine in the night
stirred with the lights of dazzling
and I know you are my cute angel
from the heaven of blessing.

I will hold you in my arms
as a statue of our love
and listen to your heart
for the sound of beautiful dove.

Ace of Hearts

Few melancholies of her own
My guilt! my delight!
whenever I inoculate her
She loves me best.

She listened my words
with a fluttering tint;
with gloomy eyes and sober charm
which makes me thunderbolt.

I invoked God to bring an angel
from the heaven of beauty
to the motherland of earth
as she is the lady of cutie.

There came and looked her in the face
An angel beautiful and bright;
And that I know she is my star
which not just glimmers only in the night.

Ace of Hearts

She wept and embraced my knees;
She gravitated me in vain
and ever toiled to purge
the derision that demented my brain.

She tended me in a hollow;
and how my insanity went away,
My stuttering voice and halting harp
disturbed her incarnation with pity.

All whims of epitome and sense
had thrilled my innocent heart;
And filled my heart with blissful
life ahead of lovely delight.

She sobs with rue and bewitch,
she tinted with love of fame;
like the grumble of a dream,
I heard her breathe in my name.

Payal Indani

Co- author Payal Indani is a heartborn girl with lots of love in her eyes. Heartbroken by her loved one. Still finds love in everyone. She is happy with whatever she has and also desires to be an author of her own book very soon. Love legal practices but firmly interested in reality of everything.

A Heartbroken Journey.

Year 1

It was a time where we used to be unknown friends. Sounds strange. But true. From strangers. To lovers. We grew up. Sorry. Not we. Only I. I had a great friendship with you. But then. You told me that you love me. I was in no mood to get into all such stuffs. That's what turned us into Unknown Friends.

Year 2

Time passed by. We came closer. You were like an ideal man for me. Who was crazy but was good? But then. People say it true. You don't recognize the true face of the one as they hide it behind the mask. That what actually I faced. You trapped me in net of your sick love. Which I considered it as a twist in my life. It was actually a twist. But a horrifying one.

Year 3

Long time. You became a drug for me. Which I couldn't get rid of. I wanted to leave you. But I couldn't. You stabbed my heart in every way you could. And I tolerated it. Just because I loved you like hell. But surprisingly. You made my life a living hell. I was drowning in your planned tricks to destroy me. But then. Something changed. You yourself gave me a way to leave you. Not directly. But indirectly in such a way that I never thought of.

Final Year

You cheated on me saying that you love me. And I knew that. Your lust and your obsession were terrifying. But at last. I realized. You Never Loved me. Never ever. And I never wanted to be a slut for you. You killed me so badly. That I started hating you like no one else could do. It's well said. Once a cheater, always a cheater. And yes. You are a cheater. Jo matter what how much I hate you. But besides all this. I love myself and thank you for making me love myself... You are not worth of facing my hatred. You are just a stranger for me. And I am just being happy with my peaceful life Without you.

Pooja J. Indani

Co-author Pooja J. Indani is a girl who preserves her relations like gems, she is a hard-core painter, a makeup lover, evergreen foodie and writer by hobby. She aspires to complete her doctorate and add prefix Dr. To her name.

Dil Ki Udaan

Dil ki ye udaan aaj kuch aise huyi hai
Ki teri yaad me aaj fir aankh num huyi hai
Yu to has lete h hum bhi gairon k sath
Par kisi apne ki kami aaj fir chubhi hai..

Dil kehta hai mujhse naa kar intezaar uska
Wo nahi aayega tujhe intezaar h jiska
Khwaab dekhta hai tu uske sath hone ke
Wo yaad bhi nahi karta tere hone na hone ka

Dil toota hai mera iss kadar
Koi khwaish na koi murad bachi ab
Bas chahu mein uski baahon me rona
Par pata nahi wo aayega kab

Dr Shreeja Singh Chandel

अभिव्यक्ति मेरे मन की ' काव्य संग्रह की रचनाकार, सताक्षी वूमेन अवार्ड विजेता डॉ० श्रीजा सिंह चंदेल उत्तराखंड की राजधानी देहरादून में एक चिकित्सक हैं, साथ ही भरतनाट्यम व कथक नृत्य में पारंगत हैं। ये बालपन से ही लिखती रही हैं तथा अपने लेखन के द्वारा जीवन के सभी पहलुओं पर अपनी भावाव्यक्ति से मानव जीवन में व्याप्त वेदना, पीड़ा और मानसिक तनाव के पीड़ा बोध को नूतन वेदना दर्शन दे रही हैं।

तुम आए!

तुम आए तो जिंदगी कहती है मुझसे,
आओ चलो तुम भी जी लो ज़रा।
आओ इन हाथों में हाथ जो तुम्हारा हो।
सपना कोई अपना रहे ना अधूरा।
तुम आए हो लाए हो रोशनी हजार,
जब से ये इश्क हुआ इस दिल के पार।
इंद्रधनुष सा जीवन हो गया अपना,
अब तो संग जीना हो अब तो संग मरना।
तुम्हारा साथ और ये सुनहरे दिन रात,
मन भरना मुश्किल है करूं कितनी भी बात।
पलकें उठाती हूं, शर्म से गिराती हूं।
कैसे कहूं तुमसे दिल के जज़्बात।

बावरी!

ज़रा धीरे धीरे चल री समय की धारा,
मुझे आज बड़े यत्नों से मिला किनारा,
मांगी थी मैंने पूरी हुई मुरादें,
लगता मुट्ठी में आया गगन है सारा।
फिरती इठलाती बलखाती इतराती,
यूं फुदक फुदक मैं इधर उधर हूं जाती।
लगता पाई हैं खुशियां जीवन भर की,
प्रिय को देखूं और देख देख खो जाती।
बड़ी अनुनय विनय करी तब प्रिय हैं आए।
बड़े जप तप व्रत करके ये पल हैं पाए।
ऐ घड़ी ठहर जा ,रुक जा, मत बढ़ आगे।
ठहरी रह जब तक प्राण निकल न जाए।

अंजान

मेरे आंसू पढ़ लेते हो,
मन के भाव धर लेते हो,
मेरी आहट भी पकड़ लेते हो,
फिर भी अंजान मुझे कहते हो।
तुम चंचल, नटखट ,मनमौजी ,
कभी शांत सरल बन जाते हो।
कभी बात हर एक समझ लेते,
कभी तंग करते हो, रुलाते हो।
तुम ज्योति अंधेरे जीवन की,
पथ उज्ज्वल करते रहते हो।
मेरी आहट भी पकड़ लेते हो,
फिर भी अंजान मुझे कहते हो।

छलावा

ख्वाब हो तुम या कोई छलावा हो?
समय की रेत में जलता हुआ लावा हो।
क्या है मेरी कहानी में हिस्सा तुम्हारा?
क्या मुझको शीतल कर पाओ वो हवा?
क्यों हो तुम मेरे जीवन में हो क्यों?
मेरी बंजर धरती पर वर्षा की बूंद।
झुलसती सी मैं इस संसार की धूप में,
तुम छाया हो या संबल हो मेरा।
संरक्षक को अथवा बल हो मेरा।
मुझको डुबाओगे या अब उबारोगे क्या?
सूर्य की किरण हो या काले बादल का साया।
क्या रहस्य है समय की गर्त में?
क्या छुपा है वक्त की परत में?
क्या है हाथ की इन रेखाओं में,
क्या जीतूंगी मोहोब्बत की शर्त मैं?

Neha Gupta

As one of the inspired and stimulated JRF aspirant, She has already completed her graduation in B.Com from Satyawati college, University of Delhi and post graduation in M. Com from IGNOU. She is currently pursuing Bachelor of Education from PMC college, GGSIPU. She has already worked as co - author of 22+ anthologies and Compiler of her own anthologies right now. One of her anthology "Climacterics" selected under Indian Book Of Records. Furthermore, she has started her own Instagram page which is named as itz_neha_writes for motivating depressed and discouraging people.

A Girl Too Have Emotions...!!

Yeah...
She is a girl but…
She too have emotions.
She wants to cry in the arms of you,
when she is sad.
She wants to cheer up with you,
when she makes the best out of her life.
She wants to give you a tight hug,
when you're sad.
She wants to kiss you to gave you warmth,
when you are feeling cold.
She wants to stay with you at every moment,
And wants to enjoy it.
She wants you to shine like a star.

She always hold your hand,
when you face the worst part of your life,
and lose every hope to stay alive.
She is the only one who fights with you
to make you correct.
She yelled and filled with tears
when you neglect her…
She become a dead person from inside,
But dare to keep alive…!!
When you left her for someone else.

She is not an open heart with you,
As she is bound to maintain the dignity of her parents,
And follow rigid norms of society.
She could not express herself freely
when she already lost the trust due to merciless folks…!!!
She wants to love you like a princess,
but couldn't to secure herself from this cruel world.

Yeah…
She is a girl who filled with emotions,
And you could never understand her thoughts.
As it's a mixture of positive and negative ones.
She never dare to leave you till the last point of her tolerance,
But yups....
She would when she fed up with you,
And never turn back in your life.

She too have feelings that wants to have self-respect from you at every point.
But, She will lose that...
when she loves you from her heart.
People called her a crazy one,
But she would tolerate that just for you, dude.
If she fails to get love from you even after sacrificing her own self-respect.

Then, one day, definitely...

You would lose her and left with the sweet memories of her.
She will never come back, but you definitely thought to have her back.
But, It's stupidity if you wait for her when game is already over now.

Sunita Bajaj

आइए मिलते हैं सुनीता बजाज से-
ये एक गृहिणी,नर्तकी,योगा प्रशिक्षु,लेखक,कविताकार,blogger के साथ साथ एक published author भी हैं।
उन्होंने 40 से ज्यादा किताबों में अपने लेखन का संकलन दिया है जैसे-
The swings of life अधूरी दास्तां
The phases of love etc.
आप उनकी रचनाओं को उनके खुद के Blog page abhivyaktii.org पर जाकर पढ़ सकते हैं।
उनके इंस्टाग्राम हैंडल है-
@mere_alfaaz14
@abhivyakti_kuch_lafz
Linkedin-https://www.linkedin.com/in/sunita-bajaj-397337201
Twitter-https://twitter.com/Sunita__bajaj?s=08
Facebook-https://www.facebook.com/sunita.bajaj.545

एक बच्ची की पुकार

ख्वाबों की सीढ़ी लगाकर चढना है मुझे
चांद के उस पार की दुनिया में जाना है मुझे
दिल बहुत रोता है और मन सूना सूना लगता है
मेरी मम्मी बन गई एक तारा
जिसे आसमां ने छुपा रखा है
सुनो चंदा मामा एक बार मेरी बात सुनो
लाई हूं मैं ढेर सारे तारे यह आप ले लो
पर मेरी मम्मी को मुझे लौटा दो
लोरी नहीं,खाना नहीं
मेरी चोटी भी नहीं बनाता कोई
गार्डन में जाती हूं घूमने
तो झूला भी नहीं झूलाता कोई
कोविड महामारी ने मम्मी को मुझसे दूर कर दिया
और मेरे पापा को सुस्त उदास कर दिया
मैं रोते-रोते सोती और रोते रोते उठती हूं
मां की गोद में सोने को मैं बहुत तरसती हूं
यह सारे तारे और छोटा सा चंदा लेकर
मैं सीढ़ी चढ़कर आ रही हूं मामा
आप मम्मी को पहले से बता देना कि *अभिव्यक्ति* को आते ही
गोदी में लेकर ढेर सारा प्यार करना..

एक स्वतंत्र सोच

सामाजिक दायरे हमारी बेड़ियां नहीं
इस सोच का सृजन करने वाले,
इसे अपनाने वाले,दबाव देने वाले
असल गुनहगार हैं, क्योंकि
भारतीय समाज आरंभ से पुरुष प्रधान रहा है
पर इसमें औरतों का भी बहुत बड़ा हाथ रहा है,
खुद से खुद के लिए लड़ना
बचपन से सिखाया नहीं गया,
परिवार वालों के लिए जीना और मरना रीति रिवाज है बस यही समझाया गया,
ऐसे और भी कई कुरीतियों में
हमें बांधा,कुचला,दबाया और गुमराह किया गया,
पर अब समाज की सोच को करारा जवाब देना है...
खोलकर पंख उड़ान गगन में भरना है
अभिव्यक्ति के लफ्जों में पहले स्वयं से प्यार कर
फिर अपने हुनर का कीर्तिमान कायम करना है।

बाल श्रमिक-मेरी सुनो ना

मुझसे ऐसी क्या भूल हुई जो खेल खिलौने छूट गया
कॉपी बस्ता और विद्यालय मुझ से कोसों दूर गए
पढ़ने को मेरा दिल करता
भार उठाना नहीं है मुझको
चाय बेचना फुल गूंथना
बिल्कुल भी नहीं भाता मुझको
सड़कों पर नहीं सोना मुझको बचपन मेरा कहां गया?
पिज़्ज़ा बर्गर आइसक्रीम को मेरा मन भी तरस रहा!!
मजबूरी मेरी कब समझेंगे
जीवन जीना कठिन हुआ
इस दलदल से बाल श्रमिक को
अभिव्यक्ति कहे करो जुदा
अपने बच्चों के माफिक
खुशियां इनको जब देंगे हम
सही मायने में भारत का
नव निर्माण करेंगे तब।

कुछ सवाल - दर्द के

मेरी आंखों में देखो और मुझे बताओ
क्या दिखता है तुम्हें!!
मैं टूटी हुई या संपूर्ण हूं?
या फिर दर्द को छुपाने का नकाब पहने
रहस्यों से परिपूर्ण हूं?
क्या सुंदरता मोहब्बत की पहचान है?
या फेसबुक,ट्विटर,इंस्टाग्राम में
अपने प्यार का इजहार करना प्रेम का प्रमाण है?
शायद मेरी और तेरी भावनाओं में
जमीन आसमान का अंतर है!!
इसीलिए मेरे टूटे हुए खयालों में
एक दर्द का समंदर है...
सुनो अंधेरों के सन्नाटे को चीरती हुई
एक प्यार की लौ हूं मैं
निस्वार्थ निश्छल प्रेम की तलाश करती
एक दिव्यज्योत हूं मैं,
अभिव्यक्ति की भावनाओं से
असहमत भले ही यह पूरा संसार है,
पर अब मेरे नफरतों का सैलाब ही
मेरी लेखनी का साज और श्रृंगार है

Nikeeta Das

Myself Nikeeta Das . i was born in Rajasthan, India I'm a student in commerce stream. I live in Guwahati,Assam, i love pets and along with writing i love doing dancing.

(1)

najane kitne sajde kiye ,
kitni ibadatein ki .... yeah kehkr
ki koi toh ho jo mujhse pyaar kare
jo mujhe jodhe rakhe ...khudse.
der se hi sahi
magar meri bhi dua Qubool ho gayi
meri tujhse mulaqaat ho gayi.
koi mila hai mujhe ,
jo mujhse beintehaa muhabbat karta hai,
mujhe hamesha khudse jodhe rakhta hai.
meri har pal fiqar karta hai ,
har dua me mera zikr karta hai.
koi mila hai mujhe,
jiske liye har hadh paar karna chahti hu,
jiske liye puri duniya se ladhna chahti hu,
jiske saath har pal jeena chahti hu,
jiske naam se khudka naam jodhna chahti hu,
jiski main suhaagan banna chahti hu.

(2)

Nahi manti thi mein khudko khubsurat
Jise kisi chand ki tarah ghanto tak dekh sake.
Nahi manti thi mein khudko ayaat
Jiska har pal shukriya adaa kar sake

Lekin tum the jisne kaha.
Ki...
Dusro se alag ho tum,
Bas isliye khaas ho tum.
Mujh jesi hi toh ho,
Mujhme khudko dhund lo tum.

Tumhari baaton se yun lagta....
Maano main tumhari zindagi mein
Kisi inayaat ki tarah thi,
Dua ki qubool hui
Kisi shikayat ki tarah thi.

Tum aksar kaha karte the...
Mera yun bewajjah rona
Tumhe bikul pasand nahi
Lekin un ashko me
dhule mere aankhon se
Tumhe bepannah mohabbat hai.

Jisdin tumhare nazariye se khudko dekhne lagi
Mein usdin khudse mohabbat kar bethi,
Jisdin tumhare dil se khudko mehsus karne lagi
Mein usdin tumse mohabbat kar bethi.

Khudko paakar bhi ,
Khudko tum mein kho bethi.

(3)

Tum kisi shaant se behte leher ki tarah ho,
Or mein kisi baraste अम्बर ki tarah,
Ki bas shaant lehro mein , sukoon ka shor ban jau.
Tum kisi shaant se hawa ki tarah ho,
Or mein kisi पतझड़ ke patto ki tarah,
Ki bas halki si us, pyaar ki chhuan se tut k gir jau.
Tum shant se thande mehtaab ki tarah ho,
Or mein kisi aate-jate *बादल ki tarah,
Ki bas logo ki, nazro se bachane ka karan ban jau.
Tum kisi shaant se andhere ki tarah ho,
Or mein us andhere mein jalti kisi शमा ki tarah ,
Ki bas tumse milte hi, mein apne wajud se mil jau.

(4)

Me jo bhi tumse kehna chahti hu,
Shayad tum bhi wahi sunna chahte ho.
Han....
Shayad mein kuch keh na pau,
Tum bin kahe hi meri baatein sun lo na.
Han.....
Shayad mein tumhe samjha na pau,
Tum bin kahe hi meri muskaan samajh lo na .
Han....
Sahyad mein tumse baatein chupau,
Tum bin kahe hi meri aankhein padh lo na.
Han....
Shayad mein tumhe khone se darti hu,
Tum bin kahe hi mere darr ko mehsus kar lo na.
Han....
Shayad jo bhi is dil mein hai jata na pau,
Tum bin kahe hi khud ko mujh mein dhund lo na.

Duniya ke har sawalo ka jawab hai tumhare pass,
Toh is sawal ka jawab tum ban jaao na

Farhan Rahman

Hey over there, today he is going to tell you about a incident that happened in his life and that incident changed him totally. His name his farhan Rahman, he is from silchar and at present he is studying civil engineering at silchar polytechnic. Before that he was a student of kv, he was a brilliant student though he lost his 2 years from his study life and still he is shining like sun. So, without wasting time let's start and hope you will like it thank you very much.

(1)

Zinddagi khud ek kitab sa hai, haar pal ek naya shik dek jata hai.
Kuch ishi taraha hai meri ya adhuri mohabbat ki dasta.
February ka mahina tha saal 2015 tha,
Tarik 1 tha, janam din tha unka, aur wo hota hai na school ke dino mei ke waqt jiska janam din hota hai wo out uniform mei askta hai, tho wo ai, haan beshak wo mere sath pehele se parti thi hum dhono ek hi class mei teh, lakin uss din pata nhi kya hua dill chu gai, kuch jiyada hi khubsurat lag rahi thi, school ke bacho ke bich mei sab se alag, Sab se khubsurat, Sab se pyari. Uss din maan bana liya tha, isko hi ab apna dil dena hai. Phir kya dost logo ke sath mil kar ek hafte baad propose karne ka soch hi liya akhir kar,
Din 7 February 2015 tha, sayad mere zinddagi ki sab se haseen dino mei se ek, uss din jaldi jaldi taiyar ho kar school ke liya chala gaya, haan wo alag baat hai pehele wale rath soya hi nhi tha, keher school ja kar dek kar usko pata nhi kiu nervous ho gaya tha, phir pehele ek char periods jane diya aur pura samaye bas usko hi dekte raha, phir aya lunch break, tab ja ke himmat kar ke keh diya mene ki " I love you, tumko girlfriend banna chahata hi." Jis chiz ki muje koi ummed tak nhi thi wo hogaya, usne jaga mei hi accept kar liya mere proposal. Uske baad tho mere khushi ka koi thikana nhi tha purye class ko party diya uss din.
Tab hum class 8 mei teh, p hir final exams ka time aya, har exam se pehele usse milne usko good wishes dene ke liya school mei jaldi chala jata tha, usko wish kare bina mera exam acha nhi jayga esa manna tha mere uss waqt (wo hota hai na bacho wala pyaar and bachpan ka pyaar kafi masum hota hai),
Phir hum class 9th mei aye, saal gujar ne ko hua, aur peheli bhar humare relationship ke baad uska jaman din ane wala tha, mai kafi jiyada excited usko suprise dene ke liya tho lag gaya mai taiyari mei uske suprise ke liya.

1 February 2016, akhir kar agyaa wo din jiska muje kafi dino se intehzer tha, phir se lunch break ka time aya, mere dosto ne usko class se bahar le gaye, thora time baad jab wo ai class mei tho suprise ho gai aur khushi ke mare muje hug kiya aur rone lagi, phir humne mil kar cake kaata aur class ke sab bacho ko diya. Sab kuch Katam ho gaya tha akhir mei wo phir se mere pas ai, mere hath ko pakra aur bola " thank you very much, esa peheli bhar kisi ne kiya hai mere liya, I love you alot," ya bol kar muje tight sa hug diya aur kiss vi diya Phir uske sath rhete rhete kab dho saal gujar gaya pata vi nhi chala.

10th ke baad ab agaya tha humare future ka decision lene ka time. Mene decide kiya mai kv mei hi rahunga aur usne decide kiya ki wo college join karegi. Humne ek dusre ki decision ki respect ki aur nikal pare zinddagi ke naye safar ki aur.

Bhale hi humara school college badal gaya tha, lakin hum mohabbat ek dhusre se khub karte teh. Mera school 2:30 pm katam hota aur uska 3:00 PM ko tho mai jaldi se ghar ja kar kapre badal kar uske college ke liya nikal lete bina kuch khaya piye, phir usko ghr chor kar akar kuch khata. Aur parai mei lag jata. Ese karte karte 2017 ka wo saal adha gujar gaya, phir pata nhi kiu hum dhono ke bich fasle ane lagye. Wo mujse aur mai usse dhur hone lagye. Keher mera jaman din agaya tha dekte dekte November 30 2017 ka wo kambkat din tha, Sab kuch sahi hi chal raha tha mere birthday party mei ki najane kiu humne jagra kar liya, gusse mei wo apne ghar chali gai aur mai apne. Samko usse baat karne ki k hosis ki magar wo baat nhi karna chahati thi. Phir achanak rath ko uska message aya :-

"Jaan dekho I need to talk with you, humara koi future nhi hai, tum Muslim ho aur mai hindu , humare parivaar wale kavi nhi manengye humara ya rista tho humhe ya yahi ka tam karna parega I'm sorry..." ya Keh kar mai kuch bolu ushe usne muje block kar diya,

Agle ek hafte tak mene usse baat karne ki kosis ki magar nhi ho pai. Ek hafte baad kuch esa hua jisne mera zindagi badal kar rak diya.

Ek hafte baad muje mere dosto se pata chala ki wo new relationship mei chali gai. Ya suun ke baad mai andhr se pura tuth sa gaya. Mene na jane kya kya nashe karne suru kar diye aur khud ko katam karne ke sho tarike dhunta rheta tha. Phir ya sab mei dho saal aur gujar gaye mei depression me i puri tara se achuka tha, Muje ab ya zinddagi aur nhi jini thi, magar jab vi marne ka khayal ata tho meri maa ka wo muskurata hua chera samne ajata aur mai piche hath jata. Akhir kar 2017 aur 2018 depression se gujarne ke baad, 2019 mei memes aur family ke support se mai phir se jine laga apni zinddagi. Aur aj mai polytechnic mei 3rd Sem ka civil engineering student hu. Zinddagi ke iss safar mei ya ek ese kahani hai jisko mai kavi nhi bhul paunga.Haan beshak yaad tho aj vi bohot ati ho magar ab tumse koi wasta nhi, jitne shiddat ke sath mohabbat kiya utne hi shiddat ke sath aj nafrat karta hu tumse.

Ya kuch alfaz hai mere taraf se:-

"Likha jo sach kaagaz par
Shayari baan gayi,
Pyaar jo kiya chehra dek kar
Mohabbat baan gayi,
Dua jo maangi tumari khairiyat ki
Ibadath baan gayi,
Nasha jo kiya tumari yaado mein
Addath baan gayi,
Ikraar kar ke meri jhooti muskurahat
Hasi baan gayi,
Zinddagi se dhur karne tumhe nikle teh
Zinddagi baan gayi."

Nikhil Jain

निखिल जैन, एक नवयुग के लेखक हैं, जो की धुले, महाराष्ट्र से संबंध रखते है। ये अपना ज्ञान दूसरो के साथ साझा करना, यात्रा करना, नई नई खोज करना और रचनात्मकता का बेहद शौक रखते है। इन्हें लिखना पसंद है, और इनका मानना है, कि लेखन से हम अपनी आंतरिक भावनाओं का भली भांति बखान कर सकते है। ये 20 से अधिक पुस्तकों के संकलनकर्ता रह चुके है और इनका स्वयं का एक ऑनलाइन प्रकाशन "unite publication"
भी है। इनसे जुड़ने के लिए आप संपर्क कर सकते हैं

इंस्टाग्राम : @love.vibes143
ईमेल -love.vibes143@outlook.com

मेरे सपनों की दुनिया

मेरे सपनों की दुनिया ऐसी हो,
जिसमे खुशियाँ ही खुशियाँ बसती हो,
जहा होता बड़ों का मान सम्मान हो,
जहा किसी के दिल में ना कोई अभिमान हो,
जहा मोहब्ब्त में गलतफहमी की आहट ना हो,
जहा दोस्ती में कोई शक ना हो,
जहा हर पल इश्क की आजमाइश हो,
जहा अपनों को पहले तवज्जो देते हो,
जहा बेटा–बेटी में कोई अंतर ना हो,
जहा स्त्री पुरुष का बराबर अधिकार हो,
जहा अतिथि को भगवान माना जाता हो,
जहा भाई भाई पर जान छिड़कते हो,
जहा गरीब अमीर में कोई भेद ना हो,
जहा ऊंच नीच का रोष ना हो,
जहा सब स्वस्थ निरोगी हो,
जहा पर सृष्टी हरी भरी हो,
जहा काले और गोरे रंग का कोई अंतर ना माने,
जहा गुरु का परमेश्वर मानकर सर्वप्रथम जाने,
जहा सब एक दूसरे से प्यार करते हो,
जहा हमसे कोई रूठता नही हो,
सपनों की दुनिया थोड़ी अजीब सी लगती है,
जैसे भी होती है पल भर की दुनिया लेकिन हमें खुश कर देती है...

"आज भी वो पल याद है मुझे"

जब देखा था तुझे पहली पहली बार,
वो नज़रों के वार, वो तेरा दीदार,
काली घनी जुल्फें, चेहरे पर आते बाल,
मृगनयनी सी आंखों में कजरे की भरमार,
गुलाबी आठ और तेरे गोरे गोरे गाल,
तेरी कमर का वो तिल और मदहोश चाल,
आज भी याद है मुझे वो पल,
जब देखा था मैंने तुझे पहली पहली बार।

मोहित हो गया था में देख तेरा रूप,
बरखा सी लग रही थी मुझे कड़ी धूप,
खड़ा सा रह गया मैं और मेरा तन,
चुरा ले गई थी तू मुझे और मेरा मन,
एक ही आरज़ू एक ही तम्मना थी,
की पा जाऊ तुझे, या तेरा हो जाऊ,
बता तू ही कैसे मैं इस दिल को समझाऊं।।

आँसू.

कभी दिन में रुलाते है ये आँसू,
कभी रातों की नींद उड़ाते हैं ये आँसू,
कभी गम को हल्का कर जाते है ये आँसू,
तो कभी खुशी में भी बह जाते है ये आँसू,
कभी अपनों को पास ले आते है ये आँसू,
तो कभी गेरो को अपना बनाते है ये आँसू,
यादों की तड़प को बहलाते है ये आँसू,
तो कभी अपनों के नकाब उठाते है ये आँसू,
कभी हौसला देकर हिम्मत देते है ये आँसू,
तो कभी फासले मिटा देते है ये आँसू,
महफ़िल में नयनों में दफन हो जाते है ये आँसू,
तो तन्हाई में बिना पूछे ही बरस जाते है ये आँसू, मुस्कराहट से
ज्यादा अपने होते है ये आँसू,
सच में बड़े कमाल के होते ये आँसू..

Moaliba Singh

A being finding new faces at these 360 universes and graces our time. Apart from such dilwala lines noting down poems in my 10inch diary, a header for biking, travelling will be noted down too, bio chalteh rahega so as life and time too.

Feels Ecstasy

Wonder why she comes unknowingly,
stopping deep breath in my soul.
Forwarding all my needs with all her deeps.
As refreshed by all her touch, wiping sorrows.
Estimating the power given by the god.
Strong she holds, more the feels grow.
One glance of her, made 'I 'thy to peace,
and there is no other for whom my tone would glow
As you're the one I am? to feel?

Soon will reach out for strong and perfect soul.
Being of yours, I imagine how I am made for thee.
Lucky am I, how I supposed to be,
coz you're the one which made me feel to it.
Great pleasure it makes me feel,
when I touch your strong faith hands.
You're the one I love the best and
a kiss of yours which makes me faint...

(2)

The piece of cake
Lights came in, she didn't
Summer dropped in, she didn't
Monsoon came in she didn't
Winter comes over, but she didn't

Delilah, not much hours left,
to build your room in me
and who's gonna have the piece of cake, aren't you?

The drunk man screamed on, she didn't
Neighbors wished on every occasions, she didn't
Troopers saluted every unknown faces , but she didn't
Santa gifted gingerbread, she didn't
December went on with lights, sweets and dishes,
lovely beings finally wished on new year eve, but she didn't

Delilah, not much hours left,
to build your room in me,
and who's gonna have the leftover piece of cake ,aren't you?

Bhumi Maheshkumar Gupta

Bhumi Gupta from Surat (Gujarat). Final year student of Degree Engineering.

(1)

कुछ अलग है शख़्सियत मेरी,
जिनसे में जानी जाती हूँ!
नाम है भूमि गुप्ता मेरा,
Mystery से अक्सर पहचानी जाती हूँ!

(2)

चाँद से है यारी कुछ बरसो पुरानी,
आओ बताऊ हमारी कहानी.!

चाँद की नाराज़गी आज समझ आई,
नासमझ थी में ना समझ पाई.!
सितारों की बैमानी आज नज़र आई,
नासमझ थी में ना समझ पाई.!

चाँद से हुई थी दोस्ती जिस दौर में,
सितारों से हुई थी मुलाकात उसी मोड़ पे.!
बेपनाह किस्से हमारे हो गए,
गवाह दोस्ती के सितारे हो गए.!
जान ली सारी कमजोरी,
देखो तो सितारो की चोरी.!

सिर्फ मुझे पाने के लिए,
वो चाँद से हुआ बेवफा.!
मेरी ख्वाहिशें पूरी करने,
वो एक पल में टूट पड़ा.!
हैरान था देख सितारो की बेवफाई,
फिर भी ना चाही उसने कभी कोई सफाई.!
कुछ तो है उससे राबता,
जो मोड़ ना पाया उसकी ओर का रास्ता.!
कुछ परेशान सा था,
मेरा ख्याल जो था.!
उसे ना छोड़ दूँ,
कही मुह ना मोड़ लूँ.!
बस यही कुछ सवाल थे,
जो मचा रहे बवाल थे.!
अब उसे कैसे कहूं की.,

जब कोई ना था तब वो था,
अब तो कोई भी ना हो बस वो हो.!'

Vrinda

She is Vrinda Nair ,19 year old girl from kerala,an aspiring writer and b.com student.

(1)

Dear naina,

I know that you won't believe me when I say i love you and i do care for you. And i know you don't care when i am worried about your safety. You always believed i loved your brother more than you. But beti i am not trying to change your assumption. Because my love for you doesn't seek validation . You were always my favourite child. I always prayed for a baby girl and when the god gave you , i felt like i had the world in my hands.

I know naina , sometimes i was over caring and over protective. And myactions made suffocation for you. But i can do nothing. I can't stop caring you. I don't dare to loose you in my life. I know you don't like restrictions and you always love hangouts with your friends. I didn't allow you at times because i wanted you to re alise you life isn't all about friends. I don't want you to be dependent on your friends , even with the family. I restricted you not because i don't trust you , it's only because i don't want tears in your eyes.

i forced you to clean the utensils, your room, made early mornings for you. I know i made your life little tougher. It's because i wanted you to be strong like your mom. I don't want you to be down with simple problems that come along. I want you to face everything with a strong heart. I want you to be independent like me. I felt so proud when i saw you shouting at papa for your right. Its not because you shouted at papa, i felt i raised my daughter with a voice. A girl should always have her voice.

Our talks always ended in quarrel. I argued wi th everything you told. We had different view about life. Even though i never admitted anything you told , at heart i admired. I was glad when you quit your highly paid job for your dream . Even i scolded you , i was happy when i saw you never giving upon your dreams. My heart was filled when i watched you transforming your dream into reality. I felt happy by knowing my girl was strong a little bit more than i thought. I was right and i raised my little girl properly.

Even in my death bed, i am not afraid of anything. I don't worry about you because i know you are strong girl like your maa. And here i am dying peacefully thinking of my sucessful daughter. I never told you but i am really proud of you my little girl. I raised a girl with a voice. Never let the world take away your smile.
With lots of kisses and hugs
Your maa.

Ritu Sharma

Ritu sharma from jaipur (Rajasthan)
Recently completed her master's in life sciences and working as an assistant professor in a private college.She have a good experience of writing poetries and articles.Many of her poems and articles are published in many newspapers.she has her own poetry channel on YouTube named Ritu Writer.Recently she got a world record certificate from high range book of world records for an online contest.She love to read Hindi poets and their narrations.She is a news anchor also in a regional news channel.

"ज़िन्दगी"

छोड़ दो मायूसियों को,
मुस्कुरा कर के रहो,
पल दो पल के मायनो को,
ज़िंदादिली से जियो..

मत रखो कुछ भी दिलो मे,
प्यार ही बस प्यार हो,
ज़िन्दगी के इन पलो में,
सुकून की बौछार हो,

हँसती हुई नज़रो के दम पे,
दिल सभी का जीत लो,
अजनबी हो कोई भी चाहे,
पर किसी का मीत हो,

सर्द रातो के सिराहने,
रख के तकिया सो भी लो,
ज़िन्दगी की दौड़ से तुम,
थोडी तबियत छीन लो ।

"मैं ज़िद करूँगी"

मैं ज़िद करूँगी माँ,
ताकि मेरे सपनों को ज़िंदा दफ़्न ना होना पड़े

मैं ज़िद करूँगी माँ,
ताकि उन सबका सहारा बन सकू जिन्हें जरूरत है मेरी...

मैं ज़िद करूँगी माँ,
ताकि जब सब किसी ओर के हिस्से मे जा रहा हो तो मे मांग सकू जो
मेरे हिस्से का है..

मैं ज़िद करूँगी माँ,
ताकि उस मुकाम को पा सकू जिसे पाने के लिए लोग सपने तक
नही देख पाते

मैं ज़िद करूँगी माँ,
ताकि जो जबान मुझे बोलने के लिये मिली है उसकी तौहीन ना हो,

मैं ज़िद करूँगी माँ,
ताकि फिर किसी ऋतु की ज़िंदगी बेरंगींन ना हो,

मैं ज़िद करूँगी माँ,
ताकि सम्भाल सकू अपने उन पैरों को जिनपे कल को खड़ा हो
दुनिया भर की खुशियां तुझे खरीद के दे सकूं,

मैं ज़िद करूँगी माँ,
ताकि ज़िन्दगी के दिये दर्द के आगे मेरी हिम्मत कम ना हो

"बेख़बर"

मैं चलती रही अपनी ही गदर ,
आँखों मे लिए सपनो का पहर ,
ओर भटकती रही फिर गुमसुम सी,
यहाँ वहाँ, इधर उधर...दुनियादारी से बेखबर ।।

किसी की आह रोती थी, किसी का दर्द रोता था,
किसी के आँसूओ के संग,किसी का रंग होता था ,
किसी की यादें भटकती थी,हर लम्हा दर बदर ,
यहाँ वहाँ, इधर उधर.दुनियादारी से बेखबर ।।

सभी को आजमाया था,सभी के रंग देखे थे,
कपट कहते है किसको फिर,तुम्हारे ढंग देखे थे,
दर्द चुभता रहा मुझको ,कहता रहा जा तू मर,
यहाँ वहाँ, इधर उधर...दुनियादारी से बेखबर ।।

मुझे ना रोग था कोई, ना कोई शौक पाला था,
मुसाफिर था मंजिलो का,मेरे सपनो को मारा था,
मगर मैं लौट आऊंगा,इंतज़ार करो पलभर,
यहाँ वहाँ, इधर उधर...दुनियादारी से बेखबर ।।

"आशियाना"

आशियाना उम्मीदों का यूँ बिखर क्यों जाता है,
ये चाँद रोज अंधेरे मे उतर क्यों जाता है,
आजमाइश कर के भी कुछ नही मिलता इसको,
फिर ये बंजारा रोज नया घर क्यों बनाता है ,

खामोश रह कर सबकी सुनता है,
पर अपनी कह क्यों नही पाता है,
गलत होता देख कर भी,
चुप खड़ा क्यों रह जाता है,
आशियाना उम्मीदों का यूँ बिखर क्यों जाता है,
ये चाँद रोज अंधेरे मे उतर क्यों जाता है,

अंदर के बंजर को सुलगना सिखाता है,
ये जमाना चिंगारी को रोज नयी हवा दे जाता है,
उठती है सरफरोश की लपटे फिर भी,
ये अपने हाथो ही उन्हें बुझा क्यों आता है,
आशियाना उम्मीदों का यूँ बिखर क्यों जाता है,
ये चाँद रोज अंधेरे मे उतर क्यों जाता है,

Shivani Brijesh

Shivani from Surat -Gujarat, recently completed her diploma in computer engineering. Doing Bachelor's of arts in English literature.

Always believing in thought "be kind to other and confident about yourself "

"पिता"

पिता अथाह रोकते है "रोना", "निराश होना ", "दुःखी होना ",,इसलिए नहीं की उन्हे होती नहीं दुःख की अनुभूती, बल्की इसलिए क्यूकी... उन्हे मालूम होता है, उनके आस-पास होते है कमजोर कंधे जिनके ,आँखो की चमक और बातो का विश्वास वही होते है । यू ही लड़के पिता में नहीं बदलते, वो त्यागते है अपना बचपना, वो त्यागते है, अपनी इच्छाशक्ति और अपनाते है एक नये जीवन को ।
इसमे भी बेटियो के पिता की तो बात ही अलग होती है, एक नन्ही परी के आते ही ये बुनने लगते है उनके लिये भविष्य की
"उम्मीदो वाला स्वेटर" बिल्कुल उनकी पसंद का,
ये कभी नहीं चाहते की इनकी बेटी सिर्फ़ घर चलाये या इन पर कोई हुकुम चलाये ,
ये चाहते है इनकी बिटीया अपनी मर्जी से चलाये अपना जीवन।
सारे सुखो का भागीदार बना देना चाहते है ये इन्हे,, लेकीन न चाहते हुए भी,, कुछ ही बेटीयो के नसीब
में आते है ऐसे पिता,,

(2)

जो देना चाहते है बिटीया को खुल के जीने का मौका,,
समाज और रिवाज को भूल कर किताबो से दिल
लगाने का मौका ।
इन बेटीयो के पिता जानते है की कितना मुश्किल है संसार में जीना
इसलिए ये सिखाते है उन्हे संसार चलाना और अपनी
उंगलियों से हाथ छुड़ा कर बताते है उन्हे आगे निकलना, जीवन जीना,
जीवन समझना ।
एसे ही होते है बेटीयो के पिता,, जैसे मेरे जीवन में तुम डैडी ।

प्रिय डैडी
तुम्हारे लिए ।

"एक ऐसा गीत "

जीवन जो इतना तीक्ष्ण है,
लिखू मै कोई ऐसा गीत.
जो पढ़ ले उसको ,बन जाये मेरा मीत ।
प्रेम, आकर्षण नहीं बल्कि,
हो उसमे ये संदेश,,
जो पढ़ ले, वो जाने जीवन का भेद ।
इच्छाशक्ति से परे बने एक ऐसा गीत ,,
जिसे पढ़ बजने लगे अंतर्मन मे संगीत ।
जिसे पढ़ ऐसा लगे,
मिल गया मन को सुकून,
जीवन तो एक फूल है न की कोई शूल ।
जो पढ़ ले वो खिल जाये ,लगे जैसे कोई प्रीत,,
जीवन इतना तीक्ष्ण है,
लिखू मै कोई ऐसा गीत ।

Arpit Dubey

Arpit is a teacher and writer. He is very fond of music and love to play musical instruments like guitar, flute. Arpit is a winner of few national level poetry competition. He is from Bhopal which is known as city of lakes. His Instagram handle is humorous_arpitdubey

शायद कह देता तुम्हे!

Cards पसंद थे ना तुम्हे
शायद, इसीलिए मैंने अपने हाथों से बनाए थे
रंग कम थे मगर जज्बातों से सजाए थे
शायद उसमे ही लिख देता।
मगर डरता था
तुम्हे खोने से
शायद, तन्हा होने से
तकिए में सिर छुपाकर रोने से।।

गुमनाम सी ज़िन्दगी में
कुछ सपने पल रहे थे
मगर पूरे ना कर पाया
शायद, बदनामी से डर रहे थे।
फिर सोचता हूं कि
शायद, कह दिया होता
तो शायद तन्हा ना होता
शायद लिख नहीं रहा होता
शायद टूट नहीं गया होता
मगर कहीं तुम्हे बुरा लगता तो
शायद फिर कहीं
सामने ना आ पाता।।

मै सीख लूंगा तुमसे

सीखने सिखाने का सिलसिला शुरू करते हैं

इश्क़ में बेवफ़ाई मै तुमसे सीख लूंगा।
और वफा मै तुम्हे सिखा दूंगा।।

रातों को सोना, मै तुमसे सीख लूंगा।
तकिए के साथ आहें भरना, मै सिखा दूंगा।।

ये सिलसिला चलता रहेगा यूंही

ग़लत होते हुए भी जीना, मै तुमसे सीख लूंगा।
पल पल मरना, मै तुम्हे सिखा दूंगा।।

मुंह फेर कर जाना, मै सीख लूंगा तुमसे।
लौट आने का इंतज़ार करना, मै तुम्हे सिखा दूंगा।।

दिल से मिटा देना किसी अपने को, मै सीख लूंगा।
समेट कर रखना यांदे, मै तुम्हे सिखा दूंगा।।

हम दोनों ये सिलसिला जारी रखेंगे

कई साल लूटना किसी के, मै तुमसे सीख लूंगा।
किसी को अपना वक़्त बनाना लेना, मै तुम्हे सिखा दूंगा।।

सांसे छीन लेना किसी की, मै तुमसे सीख लूंगा।
किसी को धड़कन बना लेना, मै सिखा दूंगा।।

इश्क़ में खुदगर्ज होना, मै तुमसे सीख लूंगा।
पर किसी पर यूं, "अर्पित" होना मै तुम्हे सिखा दूंगा।।

Samragyee Basak

This is Samragyee Basak A Graphic Designer and illustrator artist. Writing is her passion and that's why she start writing. Since then she starts participating in different competitions with a hope of little appreciation (or maybe some social validation *wink*) She dreams that one day she will write a book on her own.

Deep Breathe

The darkness , loneliness around
Imagining the childhood .. playing on the ground
scribble on the book , a handmade paper-boat
rough book ,friends, tiffin box,
colorful like a rainbow our life it was .

Now, now its gone .
now it more lack of color , like black
life now seems totally out of track ...
The things has changed over the year.
Happiness is long gone...
now its just the fear .

The fear to loose, the fear of pasts,
the fear to find the reality at last.
Those hold backs, those stories with incomplete ends
Those moments i cried , yet nobody witnesses ...
Those silences with multiple words ..

It was still the mid of the night ,
my tears dribbles from my eyes..
tired, restless i fist ...
stopping my scream of tears within

Deep breathe.
the darkness, the loneliness around
Imagining the childhood playing on the ground.

Potula Sai Srilekha

Srilekha is a CA (Chartered Accountant) final student and also a coauthor of few other books which are yet to be published. She started writing poems and quotes/shayaris from 2018.. She was born in Kakinada dist, Andhra Pradesh and was brought up in Kodad & Hyderabad, Telangana. Writing is her passion and she is looking forward to write many books in future. Her family is her strength; her parents and her sister seeing her interest and talent in writing have encouraged her to write from the very beginning.

This made her to co author the book "The Midnight Prose". This book is collection of writings of many authors. In this book Srilekha composed poems and quotes.

Visit her through instagram @srilekhapotula55.

(1)

It was painful
When I see myself in the same place even after a year

It was painful
When I realize that I could not reach my goals even after a year

It was painful
When I have to walk in the same way again even after a year

It was painful
When I have to put same effors again even after a year

But

It was worthful
When I realize that this gonna be part of my journey

It was joyful
When I learned to be strong throughout this journey

And
It was going to be wonderful one day
When I reach my destination,
When I achieve my goal,
& When all my efforts turn into Happy Tears

(2)

So many promises,
So many memories,
So many conversations,
Resulted in endless tears.....
What shall i tell to my heart which is waiting for your come back.....
What do i tell my ears which are waiting to hear you...
How do i console my eyes which are awaiting years to see you...
I hope to see what happens
If these Sleepless nights become mornings Soon
If these pains become disappear as you did
If this life without you becomes a dream
With your thoughts filled in my soul
With your memories filled in my heart
And with you filled in me
I miss you my dear.....
I miss you for rest of my life..

(3)

It’s hard to control thoughts
Its harder to control emotions
Its even more harder to control tears
If anyone is able to do the above
They might have gone through hardest things in their past

(4)

Every single picture of your's
Every single smile of your's &
Every single memory of your's

Are the most valuable things for me.

(5)

The one who hears your pain
The one who sees your tears
The one who feels your wound
The one who consoles your heart
The one who strengthens your mind
The one who motivates your brain
And finally, the one who is there with you 24/7

Is " You "

No one in this world knows that
Deep inside every soul there is a

Depressed,
Helpless,
Hopeless &
a Moaning HEART
Which is crying for the impossible to happen &
Which is waiting for the unreachable destination to arrive.

Aaliyah Stark

She is an English Literature graduate, who currently is a student teacher in training. She started working straight after graduation in Doha,Qatar for a year, then quit and came back home to pursue higher education and to do what she likes to. Her greatest dream and passion are to become a published author and she is slowly taking those small steps towards the heights she has set. She started writing when she was 14 and has continued it over the years. Besides writing her interests include cooking, reading and she is in love with music, western especially. She hopes to become a writer and a best English teacher in her future. Let's hope she gets it.

Infinte Emotions, One Finite Land

Finite, our land was discovered and built by our founders hundreds of years back. We were the best people that existed they always said, written in the pages. The only thing that mattered was building our land better, safe guarding it from the outer side and loving each other. It was hard to reach and discover our land that was protected by the gods we pray. And it wasn't just the ultimate one. We had various believers here, and lived in harmony. We were named 'Finite' because founders believed there were no other lives around this planet earth, beyond our shields and we might e nd someday. Finite land was so vast, beautiful and had various races and communities that made us so different. We had every climate, landscapes and vegetation no one can even imagine. One land was thus to make it easier, divided into states. Founders introduced proper systems and structure to make the lives of people better from good old hunting days. But then we got badly invaded they said. It appeared we were not the only ones in the planet. We were happy but we were plundered for our rich land, our neve r ending resources. It almost polluted us. But the third generation of the founders were smart and rebelled bringing all the people in Finite land together and succeeded. But we thought people in the Finite land would remain loyal. But they did not. People divided themselves on the basis of their interests and gods injected by those foreign insects. And apparently the pesticides sprayed was pretty stronger than we imagined. It harmed the minds of thousands of innocents. They turned blind with fury. There we re times they said they even doubted if this was all part of the wildest dreams. The once happy Finite land's people began to kill each other. But it was controlled by bringing faith back again. It did not work long. The fights kept going for one reason or the other. Rather the meaningless reasons were built up for the

sake of fighting. There were arenas created to put people, caged and see each other kill. But there were this two communities that was badly being preyed on. They were believed to be the peode who served the ultimate and followed their faith strongly and yet kept following the diversity not fighting back. But they were hunted down massively. The insects all over the globe helped them to defeat, the history said. How heart wrecking that could be? How more reckless could it ever get? Sadly I belong to one of that communities. And every day passes with fear, unable to imagine that one day I would be kicked out or sacrificed like a goat and that people of the once great land are willing to do thisto their own fellow citizens. And it shocks us all. We never wanted any of this. We never intended to fight back. We never wanted to see the land turning into ashes. But apparently that is what only happens, that sad fate. Why would we be the danger? They call us the children of the fire. But we are not. We are never the threat. They are. Spreading the fire and pouring the fuel around the land, literally burning everything that stood on their way into ashes. Yet we couldn't run away, strongly believing tha t we belong only here, born, raised and living for centuries, where else could we truly belong than in Finite Land.

Even with so much of the tragedies happen around me, I am still taught to be faithful to my homeland, to follow our law and to cherish ever ything we have here, without hatred and with only love and respect for the times before, dreaming that one day we would bring things back to normal, and badly wishing to turn the clock back when we were only us. The people of the land who knew nothing but live harmoniously even if it means without the technology or facilities. That bad the craving got. To be treated normal and without tags. To not be judged by what we wear and serve and to not be killed in the broad day light by a crowd for nobody's fault. To not be cheated and to be united. To choose right and to be ruled over with respect. This is what we always wanted to ask people of the Finite Land "Nothing is forever, nothing is promised, then why bloodshed and never ending cold wars. Why not end this unbelievable massacre and misunderstanding but be together? We all should live peacefully while we can and not regret after reaching hell. Because we know it is the satan that dances around."

Kamalpreet Singh

Kamalpreet singh is a budding writer from fatehgarh sahib punjab. He has done M.com and now he is doing his own business. He has a unique style of writing with a different perspective towards the world. He has participated in 6 anthologies prior to this.

Democracy

To, for and by the people government,
Its democracy.
And doesn't have any sentiment,
Because, Its democracy.

Making news from an accident,
Its democracy.
And there is no clark kent,
Because, its democracy.

Leader's continuous movement,
Its democracy.
Saying that is for development,
Because, Its democracy.

Taking everyone's statement,
Its democracy.
But oppositions always suspend,
Because, Its democracy.

Someone going to luxury apartment,
Its democracy.
All is well we have to pretend,
Because, Its democracy.

Qualifications seeking employment,
Its democracy.
No money means no friend,
Because, Its democracy.

Victims choosing suicide attempt,
Its democracy.
Criminals are on bailment,

Because, Its democracy.

Riches getting encouragement,
Its democracy.
Others have to line up in bank,
Coz' Its democracy.

Rights comes with engagement,
Its democracy.
Abusing is worse than punishment,
Because, Its democracy.

Pak and Kashmir attachment,
Its democracy.
Corruption is a talent,
Because, Its democracy.

Washing black money like detergent,
Its democracy.
Drugs don't need account statement,
Because, Its democracy.

G.S.T. Killing a merchant,
Its democracy.
Everything will be permanent,
Because, Its democracy.

Amit Kumar Paswan

Love to write
An Engineer
An Athlete
Football lover

(1)

Ham badale bhot..
Ki badalate hi rhe..
Unse milana milaana chalate hi rhe..
Phir bhi Ham akele bhot...
Ki bhot akele hi rhe...
khwaab to the ki ek hi hoga thikana,,
Par paas hoke bhi duri khalate hi rhe..

(2)

Wo khojate rhe naya mujh me,,
Main purana tha purana hi mila...
Bahuto ko pasand nhi hun main,,
Sayad kuch ko hi khajana mila..

(3)

Charag umid ka jalaye uske,,
Kya se kya kar liya khud ko...
Tinka tinka bechha apna,,
Or Kharcha kar diya khud ko...

The Mind

I am not immortal
I have no emotions
No pains no wounds
No needs of lessons
I am not you
I don't need any precautions.

Have a good day,
My dear heart

Uddhav Kanhai

"Art Is the Antedote"

Today I have a topic, one's beyond mind
That man could be jailed similar to this kind

This strain of virus had contracted our movement,
The time has come to live in the moment.

'Go Inside" is the slogan which doctors are trying to teach,
The same slogan philosophers have been saying from ages in their speech.

People got so occupied that they forgot their passion,
This idleness will take them to their unknown attraction.

Parents who stopped their children from following art,
Music, painting, poetry i s what keeping them alive in their heart.

Big businesses are shut, and art is now rewarded,
Film, books and playlist are what keeping their day sorted.

The temple mosque and church are temporarily closed,
God came forth as a doctor in need for those.

We pray for dead by saying rest in peace,
I urge people who are alive to create in peace.

The run behind the money is all at rest,
Bring art home and make it your guest.

It is time to open that box which is labelled as 'Someday',
I think that day has come and it is today or this day or this very day.

The box does not contain what the body needs,
It contains a plan, a fantasy, a dream for which we truly breathe.

Art is the garden where emotions play,
Anger, sadness, passion are malleable as clay.

The art pulls the viewer from the world of logic to the imagination,
In this process, it heals you in your fascination.

Canadian doctors are the first to prescribe art to their patients,
Make sure that the train of your thought stops at art's station.

As humans are caged the pain of animals could now be felt
An initiative was taken for the zoo culture to melt.

Flora and fauna after years are now healing,
Since the man came and we started stealing.

This virus, not one but had different motives.
Realization was one of them, which was surely coated.

I believe this virus will soon depart,
Where the heart contains love and art.

Shrawasthi Sontakke

Shrawasthi Bandu Sontakke is a student.
As like the flower blooms and sets a sweet smile to the face she wanna be the same smile giver ....
In this life span she wants to be the part of evolving medical science, loves to read, write and travel
Sometimes go crazy to be young little poet

Brook Or Brine

Be like a sea deep, still and silent
Instead of being like a river which is shallow, flowy and noisy
Because being extrovert to everyone makes you the medium of jest...

Hope With First Light

The sun rises and sets every day,
An unbroken cycle of hope,
An awakening of expectations...
A ray to complete your dreams,
A way to get accommodated in every situation ....
Getting back & moving forward with every fall,
Brightening like a burning sun,
At the end of the day dooming to the bed with a twinkling eyes to start up tomorrow again....

This Or That

It IS BETTER TO HAVE

Self love ....
Sometimes being selfish ...
Taking care of yourself ...
Thinking of your hardwork...
Thinking of your mistakes....

THAN

Loving others ....
Always being helping hand ...
Taking care of others ....
Thinking of your failure...
Thinking of your good deeds

Dedi - Dreams

Hard work doesn't feel like hard work when
When your are loving your work
When you are interested in it .
When you are giving your hundred percent...
When you are trying to improve in every stage to give your best ...
When you dream to be best in it.
When your day starts and ends while working for it

Riya Shailendrasingh Thakur

"she like to keep a positive attitude."

Akhir Tum Q Itne Dil Ke Pass Ho?

Akhir tum q itne dil k pass ho ,
Koi wajah jarur hai jo itne khas ho.

Aacha lgta hai meri parwah karna tera ,
Mere Ruth jane par manana tera.

Mere dil k karib walo mein sabse pahela nam tumhara hai,
Lagta hai humara pichle janam ka koi nata hai .

Wo waqt kaise bhul jau jo tumhare sath bitaya tha ,
Tumhare sharmili aadao ne jo hume tumhara diwana bnaya tha.

Wo masti majak apni wo mera roothna tera manana,
Mere roote chere pr har baar tera muskan lana.

Kahi na kahi mei aaj tujhpr marti hu,
Koi mujhse aachi na miljaye iss baat se darti hu.

Tut na jaye ye dosti bas rab se yahi dua karti hu....

Each One Of Us Is Given This Amazing Journey Of Life

It is up to us to be open to what is store.
Some of which we can control,
Some of which we can't.
We need to believe and let go as our precious story unfolds.

Firse Jeena Chahti Hu.

Kabhi tut jati hu, kbhi sawar jati hu .
In mushkilo k ghere mei khud ko akela pati hu .
Din bhar khudse ladkar , khudhi ko samjhati hu .
Raat hote hi sahem kar sojati hu,
Par subh khud ko maa ke aachal mei pati hu.
Jab sath choddete hai sab ,
Tab apni ungli papa ke hatho mei pati hu .
Aap hmesha mere sath rahena bas yhi kahena chahati hu.
Aaj phirse khade hokar chalna chahti hu,
Firse yu aapke parchai mei jeena chahti hu,
Firse yu aapke parchai mei jeena chahti hu .

Firse Mohobat Karaongy Kya?

Har jhagada mitakar ,
Mera hath thambogye kya ?
Ky kahte ho mujhzse firse mohobat kraongy kya?

Sab kuch bhula kar ,
Mujhe dobara apna bnaongy kya?
Kya kahte ho mujhse firse ek baar mohobat krongy kya?

Kadam se kadam milakar
Chalne ka Jo Wada Kiya tha ,
Ha tut chuka tha wo bhi wada ,
Kya ab wo wada pura krongy kya ?
Kya kahte ho mujhse firse mohobat krongy kya?

Jo manzil ke liye nikle the sath mein hath thamb kar,
Ha bhatak jarur gaye the dono ,
Kya hath mera thamb kar firse sath chalongy kya ?
Bolonn firse mohobat krongy kya?

Har fasle mitakar ,
Zindagi sath bitaongy kya?

Kahonn bas ek baar firse mohobat krongy kya?

Ankit

I'm an employee of IT sector.

(1)

Samundar ne bhi aj khamoshi tohdi hai...
Lagta hai badloon ne aj fir yaadein moori hai...
Kuch iss tarha se hulchal huie hai usmai...
Fir naa jane in badloon ne konsi baat choori hai....

(2)

समुंद्र ने भी आज खामोशी तोड़ी है।।।
लगता है बादलों ने फिर यादें मोड़ी है।।।
कुछ इस तरह हलचल हुई है उसमें ।।।।
फिर ना जाने इन बादलों ने कौनसी बात छोड़ी है।।।

Neeraj Baswal

Khamma Ghani Here is Neeraj Baswal from Delhi which is not only Capital but also called the Heart of India
He just wants to present his first love to you his Writing
He has nothing much more except of his name and Poetry so he is going to introduce his self with some writeups, hope you will like them

My Mother

The finest star of my life is my mother

Sometimes she care sometimes she cry
She was the only one who took stand for me when I was wrong or I was right
Doesn't matter I'm her son so she can lie

But only for me not for others as I'm her dear son

It was literally a huge loss when she left me alone in this world without any support but full of responsibilities of home and future
Where I'm still trying to give my best yes sometimes I fails as I'm human
But I never stop my self to try again because I'm her son

Untill she left she was the first face of bravery co urage and positive waves
Just because of she was fighting for me lifetime

I was totally imperfect since I birth but she never quit with hurdles and start jumping her self along with me and she started to do for what her son the stupid Neeraj Baswal means me needed actually

Sometimes she used to say that she is uneducated, but tell me who can be the better teacher then a mother
No one literally no one
Believe me when a women becomes Mother She becomes the superpower
She starts learn she starts fight she is biggest worrier she wins

Mother is not just a name aur relation, it's an emotion which a child cannot get again in their entire life once she left

Every Mother is special every mother is bigger than the god
Why people not ready to understand that ther e is no world ahead next to their mother
She is a whole world she is a universe

When I was akid, I always used my mother's smile to keep my self calm when I felt angry
Once she put her hand on my head
It seems like god is asking that how are you my child
Whenever I cry she hugs me and stop my crying

I forgets my all worries when I saw her smily face
And her pain get the out from mind when she looks at me

It doesn't matter how mature or too much aged you are
Every child try to finds their mother wheneverthey reached or come back to their home
It's bound of relation my stupid fellows

Yes I am broken now

But whenever I remember her smile I feel so happy and pray to God
Please give her to me in all remaining life as a Mother if reborn really happens
Please give me the same world
Please give me the same blessing

Please Please give me My Drizzle of Happiness Again

My Childhood

Everyone has memories of their good and bad times both as i have
But today I wants to describe my Childhood memory infront of you
When i was kid i was very calm
I'll not say that I was intelligent
But yes I was cute I was innocent
Like other kids are
I was much poor in studies
But Little hobby of sketch and painting I had in childhood
Which i use to fulfil my blank life with lots of colours
I had my Mother also, I want to clear you that my mother was the most beautiful face of my childhood life and no body can replace her
She was very supporting, she always took the stand for me
No doubt that i am nothing without my loving mother
Whenever I used to delay for school she used to get angry
I used to enjoy torturing my mother a lot, like play and spending too much time in streets

In my childhood I was a Tom and Jerry fan
I always wish to be someone's Jerry of solid friendship

When I was nine-year-old, I really thought that the dinosaurs are really exist on planet and I had to save the earth, I know some called it stupidity but I called it humanity

I just used my eyes like a boss whenever i needed the Remote of my Tele Vision, no matter what my father is watching.

On that moments i felt really scarry when my sister ask me to solve sums of Math which was not in my blood a little
But even then I love to remember my childhood

Nothing can match the level of feeling which I get afterhitting the ball on my neighbors window

Many Memories arounds you makes you happy my dear
Manny of them can bring tears in your eyes
It's Childhood my friend, it doesn't lies

These responsibilities seems expensive
That dramatic childhood was something else

Riya Jumariya

Riya jumariya is a passionate writer who started scribbling the poetries,microtales and short stories right from her school days.

You can check out her work on Instagram @riadorable_words.

She has won in many writing competitions. She is doing chartered accountancy course and also graduation from bachelor of commerce. She has worked in 10+ anthologies as a co-author.

Her favorite writers are rumi and Manoj muntashir.

Will You Love Me Till The End?

Will you love me forever?
After knowing about that wound that affected me deeply.
So, honestly, I used to hate romantic relationship but always love that bond which connects two souls.

. Will you judge me on every silly thing I do?
After knowing me thoroughly that I am really stupid.
So, I am not perfect at all but will love to share my stupid side with you.

Will you kiss me on my forehead and hold my hand forever?
After all I will be your better half.
So, I want you to be the the spark of my eyes and smile of my lips.

Will you let me cry on your shoulders and will be able to handle my sentiments?
So, I am very emotional person.
Even after watching "Titanic" for at least 20 times.
I will still cry the moment when jack
leaves the world.

Will you be tired of my senseless talks?
After clearing the fact that I am really not a silent person.
So, basically, I don't stop talking after I get comfortable but still, I will also listen to your stories patiently.

Will you spend the whole night in terrace just laying inside the blanket with me?
After all your chest is my pillow.
I want you to look into the sky and count the stars so that I can watch my moon forgetting all my scars.

(2)

Will you dance with me like a drunkard on 3 pegs?
After all I am a huge dance lover.
So, I have no problem if you don't know how to dance still, we will rock together.

Will you always accompany me on long drives?
As I love roads alongside nature with soothing wind which gives the romantic vibes.
So, I will totally love to drive the car with no particular destination playing our favorite music playlist.

Will you smile in a corner and will?
feel really lucky to have me?
After all I will really love you so much.
And I will be there to reduce your sorrow and double your happiness.

Will you respect me for whom I am and will never taunt the things I am unable to achieve?
After all the respect for each other is the foundation of any bond.
So, I want that we love and support each other for whom we are.

Will you always be there with me till my last breath?
After all I really want to grow old with you.
So, I will be there at your 70s like a strong stick which will support you to walk and share the arthritis pain together.

Will you be always there when I really need you in my arms?
After all that hug will be the cure of all the stress as you are my lucky charm.
So, I want you to hold me tightly and love me till the end of my life.

Shilpa Vaishnav

She is a butterfly holding the pen of love, knows how to string the pearls of feelings into words.

(1)

ख़्वाब में ही सही एक रोज़ के लिए आप मेरे क़रीब हो
बस इसी आस में हर रोज़ इन आँखों को मूंद लिया करती हूँ
मैं आपके पहलू में सोते सोते ही इस चाँद को बेनक़ाब किया करती हूँ
धड़कने जब आपकी सुनाई देती हैं लोरी बनकर,
मैं हर ख़्वाहिश को अपनी तकिये तले रखकर सोती हूँ
फिर बाहों में आपकी, आपको देखते हुए ही सुबह कर दिया करती हूँ।
इन खामोशियों को पढ़ना तो आता नहीं मुझे अब तक,
मग़र आपकी बेरुखियों में छुपे प्यार को पढ़ना जानती हूँ।
कौन हूँ? वो तो पता नहीं लेकिन..आपकी बनाई, और बस आपकी ही बनना चाहती हूँ।
जो छू लो तो खिल जाती हूँ, सपनों में ही सही मैं आपसे मिल जाती हूँ
आपकी मुस्कुराहट को ओढ़कर थोड़ा शर्मा लिया करती हूँ
हाँ मैं कभी कभी थोड़ा रो भी लिया करती हूँ।
मालूम है की अब तक आपने कुछ पल ही दिए है मुझको
मैं उस हर एक पल को चुन कर फूल से मोती कर देना चाहती हूँ।
मैं तो बस आपसे लड़ कर ही आपके मनाने का इंतजार करना चाहती हूँ।
ख़्वाब में ही सही एक रोज़ के लिए आप सिर्फ़ मेरे हो
बस इसी आस में हर रोज़ इन आँखों को मूंद लिया करती हूँ।
मैं बस इसी तरह आजकल आपमे और आपसे जी लिया करती हूँ।

तेरा मेरा रिश्ता?

तू बूँद है पानी की, मैं प्यासा समुन्दर
तू धुन हो जैसे और मैं गीत कोई
तू बारिश का पानी, मैं माटी की खुशबू
तू आवाज़ हो जैसे, मैं बात कोई
तू शाम की ठंडक, मैं तपती दुपहरी
तू सर्द हवा, मैं कुल्हड़ की चाय
तू चाँद सा शीतल, मैं तारों की चादर
तू जुगनू का नूर और मैं रात की चाँदनी
तू किताब हो जैसे, मैं उसमें लिखी कविता

तुझे चाहूं तो चाहत को खुद पर नाज़ हो जाये
तू मिले जो मुझे, मेरी ज़िंदगी का आगाज़ हो जाये।

कैसे कहूँ तेरा मेरा रिश्ता...

मैं नाव हूँ, तू पतवार मेरी
मैं दिल हूँ, तू धड़कन मेरी
मैं गीत हूँ, तू संगीत मेरा
मैं रूह हूँ, तू सुकून मेरा।

मैं रेगिस्तान में जलता बदन कोई,
तू पहली बारिश की फुहार हो जाये
जो तू मिले, मिल जाये सब कुछ,
इस ढलती रात की सुबह हो जाये।

मैं कैसे लिखूं रिश्ता तेरा मेरा...
के दुनियां भर की किताबें कम पड़ जाये।

(3)

कुछ लिखे तुमपर आज बड़ी बेकरारी है
मगर क्या लिखे कि ये कोशिश अभी जारी है

क्या लिख दे वो नज़र जो पहली बार हमपर पड़ी थी
या लिखे वो मुलाकात जो सब रस्मों से बड़ी थी।

हम तुमपर क्यों ना एक खाताबही लिख दे
कि मुस्कुराहट का हर हिसाब और लाभ हानि लिख दे।

हम तुम्हें पिरोते जाए शब्दों में और कविता लिख दें
क्यों ना ये रोज़ अपने ख़यालो में तुम्हारी आवाजाही लिख दे।

हम सूनी रात और व्यस्त दिनों में आपकी याद लिख दे
क्यों ना इन मशरूफ़ चाँद तारों से हमारी दास्तान लिख दे।

हम हर दिन के हर एहसास की कहानी लिख दे
क्यों ना राधा का प्रेम और मीरा की याद बेगानी लिख दे।

(4)

वो वहाँ बैठा है और मैं भी मीलों दूर हूँ
वो चमक मेरी आँखों की, मैं भी उसका सुकून हूँ।

उसकी मुस्कान मैंने ओढ़ी है, वो मेरी कलम की स्याही है।
वो नींद मेरी आँखों की, मैं भी उसकी सुबह हूँ।

मैं नदी हूँ शीतल ठहरी सी, वो झरना मुझमें बहता है।
वो सांसो की तरह मुझमें रहता, मैं भी उसकी धड़कन हूँ।

मैं गीतों की तरह उसको लिखती, वो संगीत जैसे सुनता है।
वो मोर मेरे जीवन का, मैं भी उसकी बारिश हूँ।

मैं चाय की तरह उसको पीती, वो मेरे हर कतरें में रहता है।
वो इंद्रधनुष सा खिलता मुझमें, मैं भी तो उसका चाँद हूँ।

वो वहाँ बैठा है और मैं भी मीलों दूर हूँ
मगर ये रूह जिस्म की, जिस्म से भला कैसे दूर हो...

Shivam Chowdhary

I am Shivam Chowdhary from Allahabad, India currently a Student pursuing my Bachelors. I began Writing from March 2019 when something unexpected happened, I am a Vocalist so just tried to get some lyrics wrapped up with my own tune and yeah I have tried to define my other side through writing, I don't write much but what ever I write it's from both heart and Soul. And I'll only say "life is unexpected everyday, be patient and spread the word of Caring and love where you go".

(1)

उस ज़माने में हमनें इश्क फरमाना छोड़ दिया, जहाँ लोगों का मन भर जाता हैं ।

(2)

वाकिफ नहीं इन इश्क की बदोश तनहाइयों से, की तुम्हीं पर आकर रुकेगा ये इश्क ।

(3)

For those who believe in True love, it's not an option, it's the Necessity

(4)

My Favourite Music is your voice, which sets up a song with my favourite lyrics, your words.

Alfiya Suroor khan

I'm Alfiya Suroor khan yet doing my 12th I have been writing from a very long time. I write when I'm happy, sad, depressed or anything it is ... writing heals

(1)

You made me fall in love with you,
How did you learn this art?

OH what better day, than
Seeing you cross my way.
I've been weaving some
Special words for you.
There is so much to say,
Oh sweetheart,
I'm in love with your inner light.
Only one glance of yours,
Makes my whole day bright.
I think about you all day and night,
And wish every day to see you sight.
In your love today,
This poem I write.
I always keep wondering,
How beautiful and kind you are.
It breaks me apart,
If I think about you going far.
I wanna stay with you,
Can't keep you apart.
You made me fall in love with you,
How did you learn this art?
I promise to you,
We will never fight.
Look into my eyes,
We have a future bright.

My Words

You said you waited forever for me to say I love you too.
But I have said that in ways you didn't understand.
Only if you knew.
And if you remember those days,
Every time I felt low.
You were there to turn me on.
Only if you knew the way I miss you,
When you are gone.
I haven't said those words yet,
Words which I always wanted to say,
But there is a feeling in my heart,
That no one will actually stay.
I don't deny the fact that I truly love you,
But the feeling of being broken again only if you knew.
So, if you are tired of waiting and wondering why those words haven't left my throat.
All I can say is, you may find the answer in this poem that I wrote.

You

I was so undeserving, and yet you made me feel I deserve the best.
I pushed you away, you pulled me deeper inside.
I destroyed myself, you healed me.
I cried, you embarrassed me.
I shouted, you calmed me.
I did wrong, you guided me.
I hated, you taught me how to love.
I was a mess - the worst of the kind,
But you still choose me,
And proved me that I was deserving,
A lot more than I thought I was...!!

Love

Baby, your presence in my life makes me complete.
The day you entered my life,
all my dreams come true.
Believe me when I say this,
I feel so beautiful and new.
I feel so blessed to have you.
You make me feel so special,
You have no clue.
When I look into your eyes and smile,
I'm carried away in them for a while.
Every day and every night I'm always thinking about you.
It's not really my fault, what can I do?
I'm happy to have a relationship so strong.
I love you more than you will ever know.
And I will always keep loving you,
My love for you will only grow.

Kreesha Kothari

Kreesha Kothari is a professional content writer in making who currently resides in Mumbai, Maharashtra. She is a diligent recent high school graduate with proven creative thinking, leadership and writing skills. Along with aiming to leverage her abilities to succ essfully fill the B -Tech Information Technology Student role at MIT Jaipur, she also has an ambition for creating great content which uplifts the intellect of the youth and also helps in the welfare of the society. Frequently praised as proactive by her pe ers, she has a great passion for writing and penning down emotions into words. She has scripted down about various topics dealing with human lifestyle, emotions, perceptions and living. She also works as a content writer for few institutes. On a different note, she has a strong wish to taste all the kinds of vegetarian dishes around the world and loves horror.

What Is Love?

Coffee dates, movie nights, exchanging gifts, planning romantic surprises, bouquet of flowers, fluffy teddy bears and physical intimate moments- is not love, but sweet consequences of the same. Whenever one thinks about love our imagination automatically takes us into the red strawberry world whose end result are boobs and butts, which is a completely dim outlook. People often confuse attraction, addiction, attachment, obsession, co-dependency and habit of a person with love, which is completely vague. Love is the only emotion with no side effects. Love is not about you and me, it's about us. It's about teaming up with eah other in order to penetrate through rough membranes and live the happiest moments together. Love is also about growth, showing maturity, sorting out problems, accepting the flaws, motivating each other to achieve their dreams and not giving up. This feeling is not restricted to a particular person like your partner, mother, father, family or friends; in fact, you can do anything lovingly. You can walk in the park lovingly, you can watch the animals playing lovingly, it can be anything just the intent needs to be pure.

In Hindi love has many names out of which one is "prem". The name has it's hidden meaning which is "PARAM" -meaning supreme and the best. True love is the emotion which is of uttermost importance and power and no other feeling can be compared to it or be above it. True love means seeing your own reflection in the other person's soul where the intellect, morals, values and perspectives all merge together resulting into birth of one soul representing both individuals. When you see other person's soul mirroring your soul, you end up loving that person effortlessly and automatically.

Parental Love

One who thinks love is always depicted by dove,
Has no idea about the depth of parental love.
People think it to be obvious and fine,
But it's the purest drug aging like fine wine.
They act like cradle for our tears and pain,
And shower it back on us in the form of love and gain.
When we feel like crashing in,
Who will we run into, to forgive our sins?
Playing the role of ladder to our dreams,
They are the one making our grass green.
One should never be scared to spill his secrets over,
For parents are really best friends forever.
Nobody can love us more than our parents from birth,
Because we are their only priority till last breath.

Surprise Wish

It was her birthday.
No contact during examination. His social media handles were deactivated.
"Happy Birthday!!" SMS at midnight cherished her all day long.

Ankush Chauhan

My name is Ankush Chauhan, I am basically from Shimla(H.P). By profession I am a Digital Marketer, By Passion am a writer.

(1)

चलो ठीक है भूल जाता हूं तुम्हें,
पर खूबसूरत रातों में की थी जो उन बातों क्या करूं...
चलो छोड़ दिया आज से तुम्हारा शहर,
मेरे गांव में हुई थी जो उन मुलाकातों का क्या करूं...
चलो माना तुमने बहुत मुश्किल से संभाला है खुद को
पर जो संभल नहीं रहे मुझसे,
मैं मेरे उन हालातों का क्या करूं...
चलो छोड़ो अब नहीं करते कभी भी जिक्र तुम्हारा,
पर ये जो रुकते ही नहीं है,
तुम्हारे इन ख्यालातों का क्या करूं.

(2)

मैं कैसे लिख दूं कुछ भी मोहब्बत के हक में,
मोहब्बत में ही तो मैंने अपना सब कुछ गवाया है...
मेरे ख्वाब तक कैद हैं उसकी गिर्फ में,
और उसने ख्वाबों में आकर भी मुझे रुलाया है...

(3)

यूं तो देखने में खूबसरत लगता है काफी,
मगर वहां हर एक कदम पर नए मोड़ आते हैं...
अबकी बार ना जाएंगे इश्क़ की गलियों में
वहां अक्सर लोग अकेला छोड़ जाते हैं

(4)

आज फिर से मचा रहे हो शोर तुम,
ख़ामोश रहने में तकलीफ ज्यादा है क्या???
शायद धड़कना सीख रहे हो दुबारा,
फिर से टूटने का इरादा है क्या???

Chetan

Chetan Sharma is a Hindi poet and has been into writing for more than three years. He is a software engineer by profession and writing is something where he gives him peace. For him writing poems, 'shers' and 'nazm' are the only things that actually convey what he thinks about life , love and relations . He has also read his pieces in op en mic events and on live shows. He wishes to be remembered for his writings and for people to understand and relate to them in their own ways, at their own times.

(1)

नहीं मिलता वहां ज़माने भर का नशा
सुकून दिल को मगर उसकी एक नज़र देती है

धड़कनें तेज़ मेरी और निगाहें झपकती नहीं
वो मिल जाए बेचैनियों को मेरी जो सबर देती है

नहीं है वादा इस रेगिस्तान से बहारों का कोई
सूखी ज़मीन को राहत बस यादों की शजर देती है

मुमकिन है न मिले सहारा अपनों का भी मुझे
फ़िर फर्क क्या मुझे ज़िंदगी मौत किस पहर देती है

जब तक रहा ज़िंदगी बेवजह हसीन लगती रही
अब देखना है उसकी जुदाई किस क़दर असर देती है

मंज़िलो में तू खोजता रहता है हासिल अपना
मयस्सर है वो हर पल जो तुझे तेरी डगर देती है

ख़ाक रही ज़िंदगी भर की तलाश यूं मेरी
उस सुकून को खोजता रहा जो मौत पे कबर देती है

(2)

बहुत दिन हुए एक इकरार नहीं किया
न खुद को खुशी दी ,तुझसे प्यार नहीं किया

किया कैद मैंने जज़्बातों को दिल में अपने
बहुत दिनों से दर्द का इज़हार नहीं किया

बताना था तुझे और कितना चाहने लगा हूं
मगर चुप रहा ,तेरा वक़्त बेकार नहीं किया

लोगों ने कहा आगे घनी ठंडी छांव है
झुलसता रहा मगर अपनी धूप का तिरस्कार नहीं किया

आएं है और भी नज़रों में मेरे मगर
तुझसे बेवफ़ा होना दिल ने स्वीकार नहीं किया

तेरी मोहब्बत में कभी मुझे कोई कमी नहीं मिली
बस मलाल खुद से रहा..इश्क़ असरदार नहीं किया

(3)

किस ओर देखा करूं मैं
किस दिशा में तुम नज़र आओगी..
कैसे सीने से आ लगोगी
किस वजह से बाहों में बिखर जाओगी..

मैं तुम्हें देख पहले रों पड़ूंगा
या मुझे देख तुम आंखें भर लाओगी..
मुझे सजाना होगा तुम्हें इश्क़ से अपने
या मेरे दर्द भर से तुम संवर जाओगी..

(4)

मेरे दर्द का भी क्या वजूद रह गया
ना तूने तसल्ली दी , ना तू पूछता है

Sonal Singh

Sonal Singh, a resident of Jamshedpur is presently completing her schooling and has been passionately working as a coauthor over some years.

An enthusiastic and a determined girl, who looks forward to turn out the best version of herself.

Being Touched

Consenting to the fact that she was 14 then,
She wasn't let out to play, for she was told " You are a grown up now".
Perhaps, a reciprocity from childhood to feminism, they meant.
A fact indeed, she thought to which she had to unwillingly relent.
She kept protecting herself, keeping herself from getting into a gathering or a crowd.
Wore loosened clothes, the way she could, so that her physical intimacy couldn't speak out aloud.
She got once surrounded by some boys of her class.

It was the games period then; the entire class had been out.
When one of them came forward and put his hands on her breast.
How wonder of a slap, a punch, a hit or a kick, when she couldn't attempt to make a vulnerable shout.

She came out of the school gate, went and sat in her van.
She witnessed some hands crawling over her thighs and above.
They were of the van drivers.
And what he didn't seem very humble or wasn't something out of love.

Coming back , she took a bath
Kept striving hard , to remove all that dirt .
Rubbing , scraping , the stains of touch , to her that could still miserably hurt.

She went to the tenant of her house a day
To play computerized games , one of the things , she always craved for .

Playing and having fun, she went on with hers , sitting on a chair.
She had to run, for what happened next , she could no longer bare.
Sitting quiet , she felt his hands moving around her waist
Breaking all the norms of her silence, she left in haste.

While trembling back her way, she was asked by someone " Is everything alright “?
Now and then a few words, yet couldn't utter anything much .
Perhaps seeking words that could explain the curse of that filthy touch .

Yet this wasn't the end ,
The time now , called upon the visit of an outsider , in his arms who held her tight .
Which to her comfort she couldn't perceive , and was left battered with a freight.

Now I ask ,
Why should a person be unwillingly touched or social ly accused ?
Why isn't it a matter of great shame for the rogues , by whom the innocents are sexually abused?

Flairs and Glairs, a platform by a student for the students. We are esteemed youth struggling to carve out our path for our future and we follow a basic mindset Since everyone is not born with all-round skills. Joining hands with people who are born to execute it with perfection is the best way to evol ve. Self-Evolution is the need of the hour but, evolving as a community is what we strive for. The initiative as kickstarted by, Founder - Mr. Shubham Shah with the motive to utilize the skillset and talent of writing has now a team of 10+ people who are actively participating into newer forms of learning and discovering talents among youngsters. We Provide platform and services like Publishing opportunities, Open mics, Workshops, Hands-on training. Operating with Brand Name of Flairs and Glairs (Publication House), we offer the chance of elevating a passionate writer to an esteemed author With Brand name Teekhe Zasbaaat. We bring to you an opportunity to get accustomed with the Public Speaking and Presenting of Thoughts along with regular challen ges to brush up your inking spirit. The newest initiative to extend our services we introduced in a new writing Platform- The Glittering Fables and Ink Over Tears.

We Choose to Fly Like A Falcon than to be

a Leg Pulling Crab.

To Know More: Infoline – 7781900870
Mail Us At-
flairsandglairs@gmail.com / info@flairsandglairs.in
Or Visit is at
www.flairsandglairs.com / www.flairsandglairs.in
Social Handles- @flairsandglairs @teekhezasbaaat

www.ingramcontent.com/pod-product-compliance
Ingram Content Group UK Ltd.
Pitfield, Milton Keynes, MK11 3LW, UK
UKHW022003190726
13853UKWH00004B/1701